JACK O' LION

A LION'S PRIDE #15

EVE LANGLAIS

PROLOGUE

"Do it. I dare you," taunted Jack's best friend, Harold, as they loitered outside the fence around the house where the witch lived. A real witch with a feline familiar that liked to sit in her window and glare.

She'd been here for decades, rarely seen but everyone knew about her. Rumor was she liked to lure young men into her house, but then the gossipers had varying theories as to whether she baked them in her oven or took them to bed.

The latter sounded intriguing. What guy hadn't wondered about a Mrs. Robinson moment? Yes to the claws.

Jack took a swig from his flask, barely tasting the moonshine. He'd been drinking since the afternoon with his buddies. After all, how often did Halloween fall on a Saturday, perfect for partying? He'd spent hours drinking and getting rowdy on campus, however, the early start led to people passing out before midnight.

Lame. As lion shifters, Jack and his friends had metabolisms that worked faster than most, meaning they could keep going when others flaked. Given the campus had turned quiet, they wandered into the small town bordering their college, playing nicky nicky nine doors—a childish prank that involved ringing a doorbell and running away before anyone answered—using up their one roll of toilet paper to decorate a tree, and puking in a bush.

Their meandering had brought them to the white picket fence and the house everyone claimed was owned by a witch.

His portly cousin Harold said, "Wouldn't it be a hoot if we scared the witch and had her like fart out sparkles or like turn her cat into a toad?"

Peter, the other friend, had snorted. "More likely she'll call the cops." A sobering reminder this could affect their student life at the college.

"It's only a problem if we're caught." Harold's sly rejoinder.

To which Peter started coming on board. "Easy enough to make sure they can't find the lion culprit."

It didn't sit well with Jack. "I don't know, dude. Maybe we should just go." A glance at the old place with its Amityville vibe—a movie he'd recently watched and been terrified by—had him hesitating.

Nothing good ever came of young men taunting neighborhood witches, especially on All Hallows' Eve.

"Pussy." Harold crowed and flapped his arms.

"I'm not into scaring old ladies," was his riposte.

Which was when Peter snickered and chanted, "Jack's scared. Scaredy Jack-o-lion."

"I'm not afraid." His chest puffed out. Because, hello, he was a guy, and he couldn't allow the insult to stand.

"Then do it," Harold cajoled. "I triple dog dare you."

And that was the reason why Jack stripped behind the hedges, not too worried about being seen by any kids. At almost midnight most of the younguns were tucked in their beds. Even most grownups didn't wander this late. Only dumbass college kids with too much booze and a need to impress wandered the night in the small town that existed almost entirely because of the college. But Peter had a point. If the witch complained, they'd be looking for a lion, not a man.

Once naked, he shifted, and no he didn't need a full moon, or even much effort. Jack's other shape, a majestic lion, never gave him trouble. It loved to come roaring out to play. He shook his head, the hair on it ruffling.

Peter whistled. "Nice mane, bro."

He tossed his head. As if he didn't know.

Tail held high, he strutted past the picket fence into the witch's front yard.

A wild garden spread from the porch to the once white rails, marking the boundaries of the property. He noted they had etchings at the tip of each, the white paint worn from the grooves which appeared darker because of embedded dirt. Weird and just more proof a witch lived here.

Pity he'd not left right then and there.

He padded toward the house, the clapboard siding showing peeling paint, the exposed wood turning gray. The shutters had long lost their brightness, the vinyl faded, and some panels hung askew.

The front door, protected by the covered porch, retained some of its color, and had the most impressive knocker upon it: a massive eagle head with fake blue jeweled eyes.

The many windows had curtains drawn across, all dark except for one on the main level, a bay with two side windows. The drapes blocked direct sight of the room inside, but it seemed most likely occupied given the seams of it glowed from a light within.

The witch had to be in there. He padded for it. The prank was simple. He'd sit outside and meow, trying to sound like a kitty. When the witch came to look, he'd give her a nice roar, maybe show some teeth, enough to freak her into screaming or doing something witchy.

For a half second, and despite his drunken state, a thought hit him. *Maybe this isn't a nice thing to do?*

What if he scared the witch to death? Humans could be fragile that way.

Some also had guns. He really would prefer to avoid getting any holes in his flesh. Bullets hurt. He didn't know that from personal experience, but he'd heard from those who had been shot. Not a good time.

He paused for a moment and immediately heard clucking from behind.

Sigh.

He moved forward, carefully choosing spots to set his paws in the jungle surrounding the house. Trepidation had him pausing again. A glance over his shoulder showed Harold flapping his arms.

Dick.

Jack had a feeling he'd regret this. But to turn back now? He'd never live down the shame. He'd almost reached the window. Close enough to do the trick. Soon as the witch saw him, he'd bolt. It should be enough to appease Harold, but not too terrifying the witch croaked of a heart attack.

Perfect plan.

Hiccup. As he held his breath to avoid a second noisy stutter, the curtain flicked. His chest tightened as his lungs screamed for him to breath. A cat appeared in the window, perching lightly on its shadowy gray haunches, head held high, brilliant green eyes focused on him. It took a second of the cat staring before it hissed. Its back rounded as it arched and kept spitting, which drew attention.

The curtain flicked aside, and an old woman appeared, her face wrinkled, her shoulders rounded. A shawl was draped over her shoulders. Fragile looking, and he went immediately sober in contrition. This wasn't a nice prank to be playing on a senior.

Before Jack could flee, her milky gaze fixed in his direction, and her lips tilted into a smile that shifted her wrinkles in a startling fashion.

"What a pretty kitty," she crooned, clapping her hands.

He didn't know how he could hear her so clearly despite the window being closed. Nor did he like how she appeared so delighted to see a lion in her garden. She didn't seem frightened in the last bit.

Behind he heard Harold exclaim, "Oh no, a lion. Eek. Run for your life."

The exaggeration had him rolling his eyes as he glanced back at his friend, while Peter chuckled. The two of them were having way too much fun at his expense.

Jack faced the window and did a double take at the cat sitting on the ground still eyeing him. While he'd been glaring at his friends on the sidewalk the old lady somehow opened the bay window. Like, how? He saw nothing in the opening. Odd since he didn't think those big plates of glass could be shifted once in place. The opening explained the cat being outside but not the fact it didn't piss itself and run. While memes liked to pretend to the contrary, in the real world, small kitties were terrified of the big ones. Blame their tribal memory of being squeak toys and snacks for cubs back in the day.

The woman leaned out the open window. "Well, hello there, kitty. I'm Glinda. How nice of you to visit. It's been so long since anyone's been by to trick me. I've missed the company."

The loneliness in the words hit him. Being alone must be horrible. Not something he'd ever have to worry about. Between his clingy mother and the lion's pride he belonged to, he'd never want for companionship.

She reached out a hand and crooned, "Here, kitty, kitty."

The indignity of it. As if he'd answer to such a childish call. The chuff of disdain he emitted didn't stop his paws from moving forward. He took two paces toward the window before he dug in and forcibly stopped himself.

What was happening? It was as if he hadn't controlled his limbs for a moment.

"I said, here kitty, kitty." The old lady sang the words and he'd have sworn they wrapped around him, dragging him forward a few more steps.

It had to be magic, a spell of some kind, forcing him to obey. He sought to pull away, to veer and leave this strange place. Even drunk he recognized something was amiss.

A little too late.

The invisible bands around him tightened and drew him to the woman who somehow stood outside. When had she clambered out? Did it matter?

She crooned, "Such a big kitty. Pity you didn't come around twenty years ago. We could have had such fun, you and I. I used to be rather nimble in my heyday."

Wait, did she imply...

He gagged.

"Oh, you think that's bad? Wait until you want me as I am now because it's all you can get."

What was that supposed to mean?

"Here, kitty, kitty."

The soft whisper drew him forward as if he slid on ice. He halted before the woman—the witch with her gray hair floating around her, a glow outlining her frame. She reached out and placed a hand on his head, a simple touch as she muttered gibberish, some kind of language he didn't understand. Weird but also scary because as she garbled, her hand heated, searing the skin of his forehead, burning along his synapses, sending him to the ground in convulsions.

Distantly he heard Harold yelling and Peter uttering high, piercing yells.

And then the noise—and pain—abruptly ceased.

Most likely because he'd passed out.

When Jack did recover, he found himself naked in an overgrown garden with the sun rising in the east. *Oh crap.* A crap that doubled when he couldn't find his clothes in the bushes. He'd have to do the sprint of streaking shame back to his dorm and hope no one saw him.

A glance at the witch's house showed it looking even sadder than he recalled the night before. What had happened? A haze hung over his memories. Bloody booze. He knew better than to drink Jager after beer.

He rose and stretched, his fingers patting his forehead as he suddenly recalled it being on fire. Nothing felt out of place or painful. A glance down showed his young, muscled body looking fine and unmarked. Even better, no cops. Also, no friends. Those jerks left him behind!

He'd be having words with them.

Jack strolled for the gate in the picket fence, took one step out, and turned into a lion. That gave him pause. Usually, he had to make some kind of effort to shift. Now he had to decide if he should keep heading for the college in his majestic form, or as a naked man. The latter seemed a better idea. Lions weren't common compared to naked college students.

Okay then.

He tried to flip shapes. Nothing happened. He frowned and concentrated. Not even a quiver. Was he still drunk? Shouldn't matter as it shouldn't have affected his ability.

A distant hum showed a car at the top end of the street. As a shifter, the rule taught to them young was not to cause a panic. He jumped into the front yard and its overgrown garden, ready to land in a low crouch only to exclaim as he hit the ground dick first because he was naked and in the flesh. His face pressed against something green and tickly, but he didn't dare move until the car passed. Only then did he sit up and look at himself. Back to being human Jack.

Maybe he'd had a delayed shift. Never heard of it but could be because it was rare. He rose and headed for the gate once more, hit the sidewalk, and... lion.

Garden, naked man.

Sidewalk—

Rawr!

The realization he'd shifted the moment he set foot off the property had him expressing his frustration. He stomped back into the garden just as the front door opened. The witch from the night before, wearing a pink house coat over a nightgown, frowned at him.

"Do you mind not making that noise? I don't need the neighbors whining on my doorstep."

Seeing her had him jabbing a finger in her direction. "You cast a spell on me."

Rather than deny it, she smirked. "Happy Halloween. Guess I know who's better at tricks."

And with that, his curse began.

CHAPTER ONE

Being called into the lion king's office didn't rattle Harper one bit. She was acquainted with Arik, a tough but fair pride leader. The golden child had grown into an impressive leader, one now married with heirs, and ridiculously successful. Some would argue he'd inherited his wealth, but the truth? He took an average business and turned it into an empire.

All that to say, she had mad respect for the king, who insisted people call him Arik unless in format settings. She wondered what he wanted with her.

As a travel nurse, she didn't spend much time in the Pride condo complex. Her small bachelor pad was more a spot to keep her extra stuff than a home. The carpet was pristine, the fridge like new since it rarely held food. The closet was mostly bare since the few clothes she had she usually brought with her.

Upon arriving at her apartment, she'd eyed her

empty cupboards and decided she'd live on takeout while she stayed. Currently between jobs, she'd chosen to take a few weeks off since her cousin insisted on having a baby shower—despite the fact this would be her third kid.

Marriage and babies were not things Harper particularly cared for. At almost forty, she had no interest in settling down and popping out cubs. She liked the freedom to go where she wanted when she wanted. Not to mention, most men bored her. The truly alpha ones were already taken. Most of the others were intimidated and cowed into a beta state around her. And then there were the ones who wanted to make little versions of themselves.

Blech. She'd never had the maternal instinct. Her idea of perfect children were the ones she got to see do cute things for a few hours and then went home with their parents. It didn't make her cold, just not interested. She felt the same way about pets.

Being alone didn't bother Harper. She liked to sprawl across her bed, hated sharing food, and got along perfectly well with her vibrator. She vacationed when she wanted and didn't have to worry about anyone else imposing on her or making her do things like snorkel or hike. She worked on her feet in her job and her idea of a vacation involved only doing things that took no effort.

Entering the king's office, she offered a slight curtsy and a smile for the man standing in the middle of the room with three golden-haired children currently using him as a jungle gym. A blonde girl in a pink romper finished climbing his arm to sit on his shoulders, chirping, "I win!" A boy with tufted locks and a dinosaur patterned shirt climbed King Arik's leg, huffing, "No fair," while the littlest one remained cradled in Arik's arm, grabbing for his blond beard.

"Hey, Harper." Arik offered a casual greeting. "Thank you for coming. Have a seat." He stiffly walked to his desk, the child clinging to his leg giggling in delight as he got carried along. Arik sat in his chair, baby tucked on one half of his lap, the child on his shoulder sliding down to occupy the other. As for the leg monkey? Under the desk making engine noises.

"You need something from me, your majesty?" Unlike the crew that called themselves biatches, she'd always had a healthy respect for authority.

"Bah. Don't you start with that title crap. Er, stuff." He corrected himself too late. The girl in his lap giggled as she chanted "Crap! Crap! Crap!" But Arik didn't get flustered or chuckle like some fathers, he growled, "Bad word," and the tyke quieted.

"Was there something I could help you with?" Harper queried, really hoping he wouldn't ask her for childcare. She preferred to stick to adults, not because she hated kids, but parents could be a nightmare.

"I know you were planning to take a few weeks off, but I have a situation that's arisen with a cousin of mine. He broke an arm and a leg trying to fix his roof in a storm."

"Sounds like a recipe for disaster."

"In his defense, said roof was leaking, and he'd hoped to throw a quick patch on it. A torrential downpour whooshed him off. He'd have been worse if he'd not landed in a bush. Needless to say, he's in a rough spot. Not that he'll admit it. Only reason I even found out about the accident is because Jack's mother contacted me."

"He lives with his mother?" And yes, she sounded judgmental.

"No, his mother lives here, actually, but visits him often. As a matter of fact, she's the only one allowed to visit. Jack prefers to be alone."

"Nothing wrong with that."

"His lack of contact with people has rendered him somewhat ornery," Arik warned softly.

"I'm not daunted by rude remarks." To be hurt, she'd have to care about what another person thought.

"That's not the strangest part of Jack's situation, though. My cousin suffers from a peculiar condition."

She arched a brow. "Oh?"

The king actually fidgeted. "It's kind of hard to explain."

"Try," was her dry reply.

The king glanced away before muttering, "He's cursed."

"Excuse me?"

"I said, Jack is cursed. I'm not sure of the exact details because he won't talk to anyone. According to his mother, a Halloween prank he pulled as a college kid went wrong and now he can't leave his property."

"Agoraphobia isn't a curse and can be managed with treatment."

"If only it were that simple. In Jack's case, if he leaves his property, he shifts into his lion."

Her mouth rounded. That was unusual. "Are we sure it's not psychosomatic?"

Arik shrugged. "Doesn't seem to be. My understanding is Jack's mother had him try all kinds of treatments, however, the moment Jack steps foot past the boundary of his home, instant furry transformation. With one exception."

"Which is?"

"Halloween. For some reason, soon as midnight hits, he can leave in his human form but at the stroke of midnight, the curse returns."

She paused to eye her king. "You're serious, aren't you?"

He nodded.

"And how long has he had this condition?"

"He's in his forties now and it happened when he was in college, so a good twenty years, give or take."

A long time to be suffering from what surely had to be a mental issue and not a curse. As if Harper would believe in such a thing. Magic and witches, ha!

She asked the more pertinent questions next. "Did someone competent set his arm and leg?"

"Yes. Our mobile doc paid him a visit. Offered him the choice of recovering at a zoo she had connections with and him spending those weeks being pampered as a lion, or at home in casts with care. He chose the latter and now it's posing a challenge since we're having difficulty finding someone to assist him."

"Surprising given how many nurses we have in the system." Most people preferred to work local. Not Harper.

"It's not been for a lack of trying. In the past few days we've gone through several aides, and word has gotten around that Jack is an ornery patient."

Harper didn't point out that, as king, Arik could just order a nurse to attend to the grumpy Jack. At the same time, she understood it would take the right kind of personality to handle it. A man like that required a firm hand and a staunch attitude that could handle bristling comments. She'd dealt with his type before. As a travelling nurse—one paid well by the various prides and other shifter groups— she provided discreet care that took into account that an animal in pain would lash out—and sometimes bite. She had the scars to prove it. But she'd also made herself a reputation when it came to excellent results with her patients.

"For how long?" she asked.

"Until at least one of the casts comes off?" A hopeful query.

A healthy shifter would only need two, three weeks tops. She nodded. "Sure. I'll help out with your cousin."

The relief on his face couldn't have been clearer. "I'll ensure you're adequately compensated. I realize this was supposed to be vacation time for you."

She waved a hand. "Bah. I would have spent most of it avoiding my cousin Darcy. She's well into her pregnancy but that hasn't stopped her from threatening to drag me in for a makeover." Because apparently letting her hair go naturally silver bothered them, as did her no-nonsense shoes, straight cut bob, and blunt nails.

Considering the company she was in, Harper didn't add that she would also prefer to avoid getting roped into babysitting Darcy's sticky little lion monsters.

"When can you start?"

"Today is fine."

"You are a life saver, Harper."

"Who is caring for him right now?"

His nose wrinkled. "No one. He chased off Becca yesterday."

"Then I'd best get right to work."

The address Arik gave her took Harper to a spot outside out the city, past fields with corn drying into yellowed stalks and the occasional cluster of cows. The small town had that cutesy feel with a single main street currently decorated for the upcoming Halloween.

Her chauffeur, the overly large omega for the pride, Leo, didn't say much. Probably because he'd gotten used to his wife doing most of the talking. Rumor was he preferred it that way. He'd been known to sit back with a beer in hand, wife in his lap, looking like the cat that ate the turkey.

Leo had always been mellow, even more so now, despite the pair of baby seats in the back. He'd brought his twins, blond tufted boys both chubby cheeked and snoring. He'd simply said, "Meena's gotta take twins number one to their swim lessons, twins two are with their aunt Teena and uncle Dmitri, and twins three needed a nap."

Even just thinking of that many sets of twins tired Harper.

"What can you tell me about my patient?" she queried.

Leo took his time answering. "Not much. Never actually met the guy. He doesn't like folk coming round."

"Arik says this Jack fellow thinks he is cursed."

Leo nodded. "Yup."

"And you believe it?"

He shrugged. "Anything's possible."

Not if it opposed science. Some might think it odd someone like Harper, who could shift shapes so easily, would take science over magic. But she believed in tangibles. The shift happened on a genetic, molecular level. A man who thought he couldn't leave the house? That was all in his head, and she'd prove it. Wouldn't Arik be pleased when she freed his cousin from his mental block.

Arrogant to think she could cure him after so long? Not really. Harper had every faith in her abilities as a healer.

"We're here," Leo announced.

The house they pulled up in front of took her aback. For some reason, she'd expected a rundown shack given the owner was a shut-in. However, the siding appeared freshly painted, the roof, despite the repair it supposedly needed, didn't seem that old. The lawn could have used a trim, but the shrubs and the rest of the greenery had nicely kept shapes. All in all, a lovely, well-maintained property.

Leo pulled her bags from the trunk, but when he would have carried them to the door, she shook her head. "I've got this. You should head back before the babies wake, screaming for milk."

He glanced at the SUV. "Good point. And good luck."

As if she needed any. Taking care of grouchy shifters was her specialty.

She gave a brisk knock at the door, which went unanswered. A jiggle of the handle showed it locked. She banged harder and shouted, "Nurse Harper here. Are you going to let me in or not?" According to Arik,

Jack had a wheelchair he could use to get around with his one good hand. So not completely invalid.

He could have been sleeping. Or perhaps he'd fallen and couldn't get up. Maybe he was in the shower, or just couldn't hear her.

The sensation of being watched let her know he just plain ignored her.

Very well then. Time for this Jack to find out why Harper had gotten the nickname of Nurse Ratched.

Because she never let up.

CHAPTER TWO

J ack sulked in his wheelchair as he ignored the woman knocking. Stupid meddling Pride. He'd told the king he didn't want any help. Thought he'd made that clear when he sent the girl packing the day before. He'd wager his mother had a hand in this. She'd been hovering again this morning.

Sure, he could have let her cook him breakfast—he did so love his daily eggs, bacon, and toast—but it wouldn't kill him to eat cold cereal for the annoying weeks it took to heal his damned arm and leg.

Of all the stupid things to happen to him. The stupid derecho that went through the previous week must have done damage to the roof that he'd not noticed. The dripping had been steady enough he'd decided not to wait until the storm ended to cover the leak. After all, he'd been up on that roof numerous times. So what if it was raining?

He would have been fine if he'd not lost his footing. He slid off the roof and, unlike the cat that startled him, didn't land on his feet.

The worst hadn't been having to drag himself back inside his house with his one good arm inside while gritting his teeth against the pain in his leg. The true horror of the situation was having to call his mother. The shame of having to ask for help. And then the coddling. Ugh. Would the nightmare never end?

The knocking at the door ceased. A discreet peek out the window showed the front porch empty. Good.

Last thing he needed was another annoying person trying to smother him. If he wanted coddling, he'd—

"There you are. I guess you didn't hear me knocking."

The sudden statement almost tore a scream from him. It definitely drew a glare as he whirled his wheelchair around to see the woman from his porch standing in his living room.

"How did you get inside?" he snapped.

"You really shouldn't leave your windows unlocked."

He frowned. The only window he'd left ajar was in his bedroom on the second floor. "You're trespassing."

"We both know that's a lie. I'm here by order of our king."

"I told Arik I didn't need a nurse."

"He disagrees. So if you have a problem with it, by all means, take it up with his majesty. I'm sure he'd love to hear you question his orders." She offered him an almost feral smile and yet it suited her.

He took stock of her appearance. Older than the last few nurses sent by the Pride, she was around his age he'd guess, forties. Maybe a bit younger, or even older. Hard to tell with the silver threaded hair but rather smooth features. Her figure was trim but shapely in her slacks and blouse over which she wore a cardigan.

"I'm fine," he grumbled.

"You have an arm and a leg in casts."

"I can get around just fine. I don't know why everyone insists on babying me."

"Maybe because you're whining like a child." Another tart reply.

The rebuke widened his eyes. "Am not."

"Says the man who juvenilely ignored my knocking."

"Wasn't in the mood for visitors." His low rebuttal.

"Is that why you sent Becca running home to the Pride in tears? Not nice."

"She wouldn't stop talking."

"Annoying, I'll agree, however, you could have tried telling her to zip her lips. Or worn headphones."

"I shouldn't have to tell someone to shut up. This is my house, and I didn't want her here. I'm glad she left."

"Are you sure she was the problem? You're quite the chatterbox." Her lips pinched. "Maybe I'll be the one wearing a headset."

"I don't yatter nonstop." He didn't hide his indignation. The very idea.

"I find that hard to believe. You look like the type to mutter under his breath."

He bit his lip before he actually did mutter about annoying know-it-alls. "Get out. I don't need your smart-ass remarks or your help."

"Yes, I can see that." She glanced at his clothes.

The shirt, ripped up one side, was slightly rank seeing as how he'd not been able to maneuver too well with just the one arm, so he'd just chosen to not change. His sweaty nightmares made that evident. Yes, he stank, but he'd not expected company.

And why was he feeling defensive? He growled, "Go away."

"I will when you can make me." She planted her hands on her hips. "Give it a try."

"I am not laying hands on you so you can accuse me of abuse."

"As if you could hurt me. I've wrestled bigger and meaner," she boasted.

He doubted that. She was petite in comparison to him. "Woman, stop being so frustrating."

She played a tiny violin.

He gaped. "What the fuck kind of bedside manner is that?"

"The kind reserved for crotchety men who won't listen. Do as I say, and we'll get along fine."

Jack scowled, but she ignored his mighty displeasure and headed for the front door, opening it long enough to drag in two bags he hadn't noticed.

She eyed him. "Where's your bedroom?"

He pointed to his left.

She glanced past him to the massive sectional with a blanket half strewn across. "That's not a proper bed."

"For obvious reasons, I'm avoiding stairs." He tapped the top of his thigh with the cast that started below his knee.

"How lazy are you?" She shook her head. "Tonight, you sleep on a mattress. But first," she wrinkled her nose, "a bath."

"Are you sure you're qualified, because even my dumb ass knows you can't get a cast wet," he pointed out. Everyone knew that.

She rolled her eyes. "Have you never heard of a sponge bath?"

"You are not wiping me down like an old person." Especially since his dick gave a little wiggle that said, *why not?*

"I wouldn't have to if you'd handled your own basic hygiene."

"Broken arm, remember?" He shifted the sling.

"You have a good hand still, all you need to give yourself a wipe," she chided.

She had a point. In his defense, he wanted a shower. To him, slopping around a wet cloth seemed of little use. "Maybe I don't mind the smell." Truth be told, he'd been avoiding it by spraying himself with air freshener, not that he told her.

She tilted her head left and right. "Where's the nearest washroom?"

"There's a half bath under the stairs."

"Sounds small. That won't do. Let's go find the kitchen." She didn't give him any choice. She grabbed the handles on his wheelchair and drove him, taking the corner in the hall a tad fast and narrowly missing the newel post. She didn't even pause for the swinging door to the kitchen. A good thing he projected his good foot and kicked it open.

She abruptly parked him in the middle of the black and white tile, not original but a close match when he'd chosen to restore it. He'd had plenty of time to renovate given his curse.

"Now, where's a cloth?" Rather than ask, she rummaged in the nearest drawer.

"To the left of the sink." And then because it occurred to him, he'd let a stranger boss him around, he growled, "Exactly who are you?"

She glanced at him over her shoulder. "My name is Harper, but I also apparently answer to bitch, cunt, fucking cow, and my personal favorite, cock sucking whore." She laid out the expletives and then turned away to wet the cloth she'd found while he blinked in shock.

He didn't know if he was more disturbed she'd

spoken those words aloud, or that people had actually used them on her.

"Have you been a nurse for long?"

She snorted. "Is this a way of asking my age?"

"No!"

She laughed. "I'm forty-three. I went into college for nursing right after high school. I did a few years at the hospital before deciding I'd rather travel and do private gigs. I get to see new places and it pays better."

"Must be nice," he muttered.

She heard. "It is."

He'd been stuck here since the curse. Yes, he did occasionally stretch his legs, but given he turned into a lion the moment he set foot off the property, it didn't make for interesting excursions. He missed going to restaurants, the movies, even bowling, which he sucked at and hated because of the smelly shoes.

During their talk, she'd filled a bowl with water and wrung the cloth she'd found.

"You can't seriously be about to wash me here," he complained.

"Why not? There's no one around."

"Because I don't want you to." His plea fell on deaf ears.

She headed for him with the bowl smelling of dish detergent and the dreaded cloth. He reached for it, but she held it out of reach.

"I'll do it."

"If you were going to do it you wouldn't reek of three-day-old smelly cheese. Your scruffy beard has crumbs!" she stated with indignation as if personally affronted.

He rubbed at the tufts of hair. He went through stints where he shaved to the skin. Then depression would hit, and he'd think, why bother? It wasn't as if he had anyone to impress.

The cloth slapped him wetly in the face and while he did his best to twist and duck, Nurse Harpy remained firmly determined to scrub at him. She pulled it away for a rinse while he protested.

"Enough. I get your point."

"Do you?"

"Yes. Now leave me alone."

"Nope. You smell and since I refuse to subject my nose to that kind of abuse, I will deal with it." She eyed his shirt, which he'd torn so he could maneuver it over the broken arm that hung in a sling. She grabbed hold and ripped it free.

"Hey! I happened to like that shirt." Not really, hence why he'd adjusted it in the first place.

"Were you this whiny as a child?" she asked as she more gently removed his sling before whacking the cloth to his chest for a moist glide.

He held on to his irritation to help him ignore the fact she touched him. It had been a while since that had happened. He got few guests. Harold and Peter used to come in the beginning until the guilt got to be too great. They realized it could have easily been them trapped.

Hard to meet girls stuck at home. At least the internet helped. He made online connections. Learned that jerking off with someone on the other side of a camera could help him not want to drown himself in the bathtub.

To his surprise, some women wanted to meet him in person, despite the fact he pretended to be one of those people afraid to leave the house. They didn't last. Eventually, they annoyed him, or they got tired of the fact he truly wouldn't leave the house. Given the result never changed, he'd not bothered to meet anyone in the last few years and truly kept to himself.

Stupid curse.

The cloth wound lower and lower, and he kept his legs pinched tight, trapping a dick that proved all too happy to have Nurse Harpy stroking him in a very clinical manner. She kept her lips pursed, her gaze on her task. Definitely not getting off seeing him half naked. He doubted he'd have the same kind of control if the roles were reversed.

The washing remained above the waistband for the moment as she handled his pits, his unbroken arm, his back, and his neck. She ran fingers through the hair on his head and tsked. "This is too greasy for dry shampoo." Without asking, she tilted his chair and wheeled him to the counter. "You'll have to stand for a few minutes and stick your head in the sink."

"And if I say no?"

"Do you really want to see who wins that battle?" was her sweet riposte.

Not really, because he had a feeling it might be emasculating. He got up and put all his weight on his good leg while leaning the heel of the one in its cast at an angle for balance but no pressure—not for a few more days at least, according to the doctor. With his good hand braced on the counter, he tilted his head as directed. He had to admit, it did feel good to have the warm water sluicing his scalp. Her fingers might be brisk in their lathering massage, but he still relaxed. She rinsed him before slapping a dry towel on his head.

"Hold that for a moment," she ordered.

He didn't think, but grabbed the towel with his good hand, leaving him defenseless for the attack on his pants.

"What are you doing, woman?" he yelped as she gave his track pants a yank.

Her tart reply? "You forgot to wash your nether regions."

Before he could slap her away or hop out of reach, she'd dropped his drawers and his dick sprang out, prouder than a Fourth of July flagpole.

CHAPTER THREE

I t wasn't the first time Harper faced an erect dick. Men just couldn't help themselves. Even the most basic touch could give them a boner. Most thought it gave them license to make leering remarks.

"Hey nurse, I got something for you to examine."

"I've got the cure you need." Wink. Wink.

She might have been less than gentle when she told them she had to check their temperature—rectally.

Jack didn't shake his penis and expect her to drop to her knees in admiration. He dragged the towel from his head and dangled it in front of his groin. Ruddy color mottled his cheeks.

"I'll wash my own balls," he said, tight-lipped.

Since she'd proven her point—*don't be a lazy whine bag*—she dropped the cloth in the bowl with a splash. "If you insist. Be sure to get between those cheeks too."

His face turned so red she worried he might be

having a cardiac episode. She turned away and left him to his bathing—and muttering. She gave the kitchen a once over to get an idea of what she had to work with. She couldn't cook very well, but she could order in like a champ and knew how to make sure she got enough to make leftovers.

Despite the age of the house, she stood in a gourmet kitchen with tons of whitewashed wood cabinets, a good number of them framing the large window overlooking the yard. They went around the massive side-by-side door of the stainless steel fridge. Even the dual ovens on the wall were surrounded. Topping them off were gray and white granite countertops streaked with a hint of black.

Nice. But a pretty kitchen didn't mean food. Some were just for show.

She yanked open the fridge to find more than expected. To the left, freezer items. Shelves of neatly stacked food containers, the tops of them bearing handwritten labels.

Lasagna March. Rice and chicken April.

Premade meals, homemade. Practical. She closed the freezer and looked in the fridge side to see more neatness. A jug of milk lined up with orange juice and buttermilk. Even some heavy whipping cream. Stacks of cardboard with eggs—the brown kind. The drawers held vegetables and dairy. On a shelf was a plate covered with clear plastic wrap. A peek showed mashed potatoes and roast beef smothered in gravy with a side of carrots. A second plate behind it held curried rice and shrimp, ready to be microwaved. Smart.

A glance showed the machine to the left of the fridge over a food prep area that also held a toaster and air fryer. Nice to know mealtime wouldn't be an issue.

"Who do you get the food from?" she asked as she closed the fridge door.

"The ingredients come from the grocery store and then the meal itself depends on the recipe."

"Wait, you cooked all that?" Those dishes were way above her skill level. She usually burned rice unless she got the kind she could microwave in a bag.

"I prefer to know what's going into my body."

A body with an excellent physique which she noticed as someone in healthcare, not because he was ripped. "Good to know I won't starve while I'm here. Just so you know, though, I hate peas."

"How can you hate peas?" he exclaimed. "They're like little green jewels that explode flavor into your mouth."

"Blerg. Peas are nasty, mushy pods of vileness." She grimaced at the memory of having to eat them as a kid. The frozen kind were especially gross.

She moved to the pantry and stared at the neatly labelled containers on the shelves. Sugar. Flour. Baking powder. Another kind of flour. An impressively large rack of spices. He really did cook.

"You only think that because you haven't tried my

pea risotto." He paused. Had he just realized what he'd implied? Yup, because he added, "Not that you'll be tasting it. You'll be gone by dinner. Morning at the latest."

"Doubtful. It'll be at least two weeks before you can think of removing any casts. I saw your x-rays." She moved on to the cupboard on the side of the pantry to discover the stash of real food—a.k.a. snacks.

"You'll be gone," he stated with assurance. "The longest nurse only made it twelve hours." He made it sound like a point of pride.

Harper spotted an adequate selection of chips but didn't see any cookies. "Where do you hide your sweets?"

"I don't. I'm not a dessert guy."

Gasp. The travesty. "Well, that won't do. I need my sugar. I assume you have someone who delivers groceries since you refuse to go out?" She looked around for a pad of paper and a pen.

"I use a delivery app for the local store."

"Perfect. I'll need to add some things."

"Not happening. You won't be here long," he replied stubbornly.

Rather than answer that statement she chirped, "Don't forget, after you do that spot between those butt cheeks give a good scrub under your nut sac."

He went silent and she grinned as she did a mental catalogue of what he lacked. If he thought her tough now, he should see her if she became sugar deprived.

"Done." A stiff claim.

"Just one more thing. Kick off your pants if you can. If not, I'll strip them. Can't be putting those back on or you'll have to wash again."

"Fucking bossy," he muttered, grunted, and finally tore fabric as he decided to not fight with the pants that had been cut on one leg to accommodate his cast.

"Look at the big boy able to get undressed by himself. Now, do you need me to help you get some clean pants on?"

"No," he growled. A creak sounded as he sat in the wheelchair and wheeled away.

"Holler if you get stuck." Spoken to a swinging door. He'd already fled.

Harper snared a banana and ate it before she went looking for her patient and found him in his living room where he lay on the floor, cursing at his pants. He'd only gotten his unbroken leg inside. He held the towel bunched in his lap for modesty. The glare he offered warmed her through and through.

"You knew this would happen," he accused.

"Well, yeah. If it were easy to take care of yourself you wouldn't need me." She rolled her eyes as she knelt with the scissors. "Now, are you going to let me help, or will we be spending the next two weeks with you naked?"

"I dressed myself just fine before you got here," he protested.

"I wouldn't call wearing the same clothes for days on end getting dressed. They were disgusting rags."

"Maybe I'll just start wearing togas."

She couldn't help but smirk. "Please do. It would make both our lives that much easier. Shall I fetch a sheet?"

His jaw gritted. "Cut the pants."

She clacked the scissors. He flinched. Hiding a grin, she said, "I'll have to remove them first."

He put his hand over his towel-covered junk as she tugged the fabric free. She trimmed the seam of the leg to widen the section going over the cast, then maneuvered the waist over his broken leg first before getting him to bend his good one and poke his foot through the unmodified side.

Next, she helped him ease the shirt over his cast, then his good arm and torso, before placing his arm back in a sling. When she finished, she got a begrudging, "Thanks."

"See how much easier it is when you listen."

He snarled. "And you just had to ruin the moment."

"Were we having a moment? Hard to tell with your scowling. Shall we head for the kitchen and have a snack?"

"Going to hand feed me like a baby?" he asked with a sneer.

"Why would I do that when you still have a perfectly good, working arm? If you insist, I'll cut your meat. Personally, I don't see why you can't stab it with a fork and gnaw, but some people can be prissy about food. Speaking of which, what are you going to serve? It's been a while since lunch."

"You expect me to make you a snack?" Long lashes blinked with incredulity.

"Well, you are the chef." He must have hit his head on the way off the roof given he'd forgotten. "And trust me when I say you do not want me anywhere near your kitchen tools."

His lips pressed into a line. "I am not your servant."

She reached a hand to him seeing as how he'd yet to get up off the floor. "Are you going to sulk? Because if you are, I'll let you tantrum in private while I run to the store and get some stuff. I'm thinking donuts would be nice."

"Processed garbage."

"Exactly how I like it," she chirped.

Jack eyed the chair then her hand before he clasped it. He made sure to only use his good foot to brace as she heaved him upright. "Processed sugary junk is unhealthy."

"Says the man who never leaves the house."

"Not by choice."

"When was the last time you ventured out?" she queried as she aimed the wheelchair in place behind him. Pushing Jack to act and not mope didn't mean letting him overdo it.

"I don't know."

She'd done a bit of searching before heading over. "Local news doesn't have any mention of lion sightings in years now." But they'd definitely been a thing, especially around the time he decided to claim he was cursed. Used to be, people regularly spotted a lion about town which led to unsavory types showing up and firing off guns. Not all of those hunters returned home, which led to even more of them loitering. But alas, none of them ever bagged a hairy feline and the sightings grew few and far between.

"Maybe I got tired of realizing I'm fucked." His lips turned down. He pivoted rapidly from her and rolled to the kitchen.

"Why are you afraid of leaving?" she hammered. "Did something happen?"

"Yeah, a curse happened. Didn't Arik tell you that?"

"He did mention the fact you're unable to leave. Apparently, something made you nervous about going back out into the world."

He snorted as he slapped past the kitchen door. "Of course you'd assume I'm here by choice."

"What else would I think?"

"I get it. Used to be I didn't believe in magic either. After all, witches aren't real. Curses only exist in books and movies." He paused by the fridge and eyed her. "I've heard it all and do you know, I wish they were right. In the beginning, I spent years looking for a way out. But the witch's spell can't be broken." He referred to his delusion. A good start to finding him a cure.

"Have you been examined? Tried speaking to a psychologist?" She perched on a stool as he wheeled eggs and bacon to the counter with its built-in cooktop.

He went back to the fridge for more stuff before he answered. "I've had doctors. Shrinks. Even let some Russian ursine hypnotize me. Nothing worked."

"Everyone sees issues differently. Maybe you've not been diagnosed by the right person yet."

"Let me guess, you, a nurse, will magically see what's wrong with me and fix it," he drawled with heavy sarcasm.

"Actually my plan is to scientifically analyze the situation as I don't believe in magic."

"Must be nice," he snorted.

"I'm beginning to think it might be because you enjoy drama. The tragic man stuck in a gorgeous house, spending his days cooking gourmet meals and watching soap operas."

"You cannot be serious." He plopped more vegetables than she trusted next to the eggs and bacon on the counter.

"Well, what else do you do if you're not looking for a way out?"

"I work."

"Really? At what?"

"I play with stocks."

Her mouth rounded. "For real? I thought that was

a made-up job for movies. Shouldn't you be in, like, New York, wearing a suit on Wall Street?"

His shoulders rounded. "Nope. Don't need to leave the house to do it and it can pay good if you're smart. How do you think I managed to afford to renovate this place?"

"Do you like being stuck here?" She changed tactics.

"What do you think?"

"If you're not happy then why not let *the nurse*"—she did finger quotes—"examine you? I promise I won't squeeze your balls and make you cough."

Jack stared at her for so long she almost snapped her fingers. He then said slowly, "I guess there's no harm in trying."

"Good. We'll conduct a basic exam after we eat whatever it is you're making."

It turned out to be an egg dish, like an omelet, but next level. She groaned more than once eating it.

"If this is your idea of a snack, I might die when we get to dinner," she admitted as she did the cleanup. He'd cooked, which made it fair.

"It's reheated simple stuff. I have days where I want easy."

"Don't we all. Now, sit down, and let's take a peek at you."

She ran a gamut of little tests. Blood pressure. Pupil dilation. Asked him questions about his curse.

"How long after you leave the property before you

change into a lion?"

"The moment I step past the gate."

"Have you tried leaving via other spots? Like leaping over the back or side?" Could be the gate was a mental trigger.

"Every square inch. I've tried to tunnel under as well. Even ordered a hang glider to leap from the roof. No matter what, I shift soon as I hit the property line."

What a shame she couldn't get him to demonstrate without wrecking his casts. "Did the witch ever explain the curse to you?"

"Yeah. It was originally meant to last one year. She bound me to her service so I could repent my prank. And it worked. Once I got to know Glinda, I felt bad I'd tried to scare her. She was planning to release me on Halloween, but only two weeks beforehand she got in a car accident. She never made it out of the hospital." His lips turned down. "And I was stuck."

"I'm surprised her heirs let you stay in the house."

"Turns out she had none. At some point after I moved in by force, she changed her will and left everything to me."

"She must have really liked you," she teased. "Did you have to put out?"

Horror creased his face. "Ew. No. She was like a grandmother to me."

It amused Harper to antagonize him, but she needed to stay focused. She was here to help him, after all. She decided to change tactics.

"And according to you, Glinda was also a witch, meaning she must have spell books." If she played along with his line of thinking, perhaps she'd find something that would help unlock his psychological blocks or prove the point he was acting ridiculous.

He stared at her.

"Come on, any witch worth her salt is gonna have some kind of grimoire." She pulled on all the knowledge she had from reading fairy tales and fantasy movies in her younger days.

Again, his shoulders rolled. "Not that I found.

"I assume you've looked everywhere."

"I've been here twenty years. Yeah, of course I've been over every square inch of this place and never found anything."

"Because it wouldn't be in the open. Duh. A witch would hide her hobby."

"Why would she hide it?"

"Maybe so they won't be found when annoying boys try to prank her," she sassed.

He winced.

"Does she have any literature at all? Journals?"

"Nothing, just a few old photo albums."

"Hmm." All she said.

"What's that supposed to mean?"

"That I do believe we've found ourselves a mystery, Jack."

And she just loved a good puzzle.

CHAPTER FOUR

J ack would never admit it, but he already felt better than he had since he'd woken a broken mess on the slick ground. The agony of dragging himself inside had been fleeting in comparison to his frustration afterwards at his inability to resume his life.

A life monotonous and predictable. Until now.

Being beholden to anyone didn't sit well. He'd made that clear with the nurses who'd shown up since the doctor had put him in the casts. They'd tried to baby him. One young male and three females. None lasted long.

Turned out it wasn't that hard to set off the generation that couldn't handle conflict. But Nurse Harpy wasn't like those kids. She had an iron core and didn't back down.

In this case, he was glad she'd proved tough,

because clean clothes and a less reeking body improved his mood from dour to less dour.

But her groaning as she ate the frittata? That proved downright pleasurable.

Her insistence on examining him? Frustrating. He gritted his teeth against her touch and hoped she couldn't see his cock twitching and being a right dick in his pants.

She didn't find anything unexpected which led to her muttering, "All normal, meaning it's not easily visible."

He should show her the many MRIs, X-rays, and CAT scans he'd had done. None were cheap, as they required portable machines and skilled people who knew the shifter secret. Few of those existed, which put them in high demand. He even left the house and had himself checked out by a veterinarian who also couldn't find anything wrong, but did say she could get him a nice home in a local zoo. He almost ate her for even suggesting it.

At six o'clock, Nurse Harpy fed them the leftovers in the fridge for dinner, then she took him outside for some fresh air. She first parked his wheelchair on the porch before heading inside and bringing out a stool to join him.

She read a book. He played on his phone. The stocks needed adjusting.

At nine o'clock, she declared it was time to prep him for bed and she meant what she'd said earlier. He wouldn't be sleeping on the couch. She wheeled his chair to the foot of the stairs and locked the wheels.

"I don't know how you think I'm getting up there." He didn't rise from his seat.

"Easy. I'll be the crutch for your bad side. Hold the rail with your good hand."

He wanted to argue. It sounded like a lot of effort. Not to mention emasculating. He didn't need Nurse Harpy propping him up. At the same time, if he let his pride overcome common sense, he could end up falling and making things far worse.

"Don't complain if I'm heavy." He'd never been a small guy. Hence why he liked good food. Exercise kept him from getting fat, but he had heft.

She didn't even grunt as she propped and helped him maneuver up the stairs to the landing outside the bedrooms. There were three in total, plus one over-sized bathroom.

"I am the room on the end."

Two doors opened onto a master suite. He'd long ago stripped its wallpaper. The carpet he'd removed had revealed wood floors which he'd varnished. He had replaced the flimsy, Victorian-style furniture with sturdy, rustic pieces that wouldn't have been out of place on a ranch. The plaid comforter and matching drapes went well with the synthetic fur rug lying in front of the potbellied wood stove.

"Holy testosterone cave." She whistled as they looked in from the hallway. "This screams 'bachelor.'"

"As opposed to pussy whipped?" he riposted. "So sorry if it's lacking ruffles and pink."

Her throaty laughter made his chest tighten. "Actually, that's equally horrifying. Your room isn't that bad. I'm more of a blue plaid than red, though."

"Are you with someone?" A casual query that he had no place asking. He couldn't have said how it slipped from his lips. It was none of his business.

"Single and that's how I like it. No offense, but men are high maintenance."

He couldn't stop his chuckle. "I would have said the opposite."

"Careful there, Jack. We're almost agreeing on something."

"Can't have that," he murmured.

"Let's get you to the bathroom to handle your business before bed." She supported him as they continued hopping down the hallway, to the space he'd renovated with white honeycomb tile edged with yellow and black. The claw foot tub under the custom round window drew the eye. "Very nice. Is this the only bathroom with a shower?"

"Yeah. Don't usually need to share."

"I'm sure we'll manage. You should use the toilet now and then wash again," she stated, grabbing a facecloth from a built-in cabinet and running the water in the sink.

"Yes, dear." His sarcastic reply.

"Don't you get sassy with me. I have a rectal thermometer and I will use it."

"Maybe I like things up my ass." He'd never tried but that wasn't the point.

She blinked. Then grinned as she left the wet cloth on the side of the sink. "Holler when you're done."

Despite it being awkward, he managed his toiletries before humping his way to the door, panting only slightly given he'd been keeping himself upright on one leg for a fair bit at this point. He opened the door and bit back a yell to find the nurse standing on the other side, his office chair waiting.

She patted it. "This will be your upstairs wheels. Sit and scoot."

He could have kicked himself for not thinking of his roller chair. He parked his ass, but before he could use his foot flintstone style, she'd raced him to his room, leading him to yell, "Whoah!"

The abrupt brake almost threw him out. "You have arrived at your final destination."

He glanced at her, flushed and looking pleased with herself. Waiting for him to say something.

"I think there's a second wheelie chair in the basement if you want to race."

"Is that a challenge?" She arched a brow.

"Only if we place a wager on it."

"Let me see the state of the chair first." She winked and patted the bed. "Up you go." She held out her hand to help heave him to his feet and he pivoted on his good foot to put his ass on the bed. It would be nice to have his mattress. He eased on to the firm yet soft surface and sighed.

"Yodel if you need me." Nurse Harpy pulled the covers over him and left, turning out the light.

A pity his sleep couldn't be as thick as the darkness. He lay awake for a while, and when he did finally sleep, it was to suffer the nightmare he dreaded. That of his first Halloween after Glinda died.

Jack had received the news of Glinda's death with shock. She'd not been so bad, and he found himself sad at her passing. But he also bad-mouthed her name once he realized her death didn't release him from the curse.

Every day he tried setting foot past that fence once darkness fell. Every day he slunk back into the house, clutching his clothes.

Until Halloween.

He'd turned off all the lights and huddled by the window. One year since he'd become a prisoner, getting fat on Glinda's baking. The woman could cook and had taught him the basics. He missed the smell of her roast beef and his favorite loaded potato soup.

Keeping watch, he knew when the streets finally quieted enough for him to do his nightly attempt. Maybe, he thought, the spell took time to fade once its caster died.

He wore a robe, the kind easily slipped off once he failed to stay in his man shape. Barefoot and feeling kind of hopeless, he stood by the fence, bracing himself for disappointment.

A step over the boundary and his foot didn't change. He blinked. He put another foot out and stood on the other side of the fence. Still not a lion.

His lips split into a grin. His curse was gone! He eyed the robe he wore, then his house. Did he dare go back in for real clothes?

Fuck no. He took off running, bare soles slapping pavement, his balls dancing under the cover of his robe. He had no wallet, no phone, nothing but the joy of being free. He also lacked a destination.

It took only a moment to decide where to go first. The dorm where Peter or Harold could give him some clothes. To say they were surprised to see him was an understatement.

Harold had gaped so long, Jack blew him a kiss. "Take a pic, bro. It will last longer."

"You're free!" It led to jubilant back slaps and ribald laughter. For the first time in a year, Jack felt normal. But that didn't mean he accepted the offered beer to celebrate.

He shook his head. "No alcohol for me, boys. But I will take some clothes and cash for a cab." Since he no longer had his own room on campus, heading home to his mother seemed best.

She'd be overjoyed to have her baby back. He might even allow her smothering as he adjusted back to the world.

He made it to her place before midnight. Her tears soaked the fabric of his borrowed shirt. When he tired of the blubbering, he fled his mom's presence for a shower.

While under the hot spray, he suddenly shifted.

And roared!

The bathroom door didn't respond to batting paws. He growled and butted it until his mother opened it with a tart, "What is your—Oh, no! Baby! What happened?"

He offered a gargled growl in reply and shook his wet fur in annoyance which led to her screeching, "Not inside the house!"

It really grated his lion ass that he needed her help to open the door to the outside. He had time to be really annoyed by the time he'd run back to Glinda's house, arriving an hour or so before dawn.

The moment he entered the yard. Poof. Man.

The next year on Halloween, he stayed up on the thirtieth and waited for midnight. At twelve oh one, he stepped past the fence.

Man.

Midnight twenty-four hours later? Lion.

Ever see the movie Ladyhawke? *For some reason it made him think of his situation only without the lovely Michelle Pfeiffer to be his Isabeau.*

For the first decade, he used that one day of freedom to go out and feel normal. Only with every passing year, he felt more and more estranged from the world outside his house. Then the year came that he didn't bother leaving his couch on Halloween.

Or the next.

Why bother when it only reminded him of what he couldn't have?

No life.

No love.

Alone.

Forever.

He woke, lying in a pool of sweat, wondering what woke him when he heard the shriek.

CHAPTER FIVE

The weight on Harper's chest confused, but it was the huff of hot air on her face and the dig of claws in her chest that fully woke her.

I'm being attacked!

Harper screamed and flailed, launching the cat trying to smother her!

The smoky gray feline flipped midair and landed on the dresser with a nonchalance her lioness envied. The domestic breed then proceeded to lick its ass.

"What the actual heck, kitty!" Harper huffed as her heart raced. Not usually one to startle, she'd found herself unusually unsettled in Jack's strange house. She'd struggled to get to sleep, the noises of the house only part of why she couldn't rest. Her mind had been whirring, consumed with thoughts of Jack.

What an ornery man. With reason. Caught in a trap of his own making. He'd convinced himself he couldn't get out unless he wanted to be a beast. Had he been a dog or a house cat, it might have been doable, because people wouldn't have hunted his ass. However, a lion? As history showed, not only did people feel uncomfortable with one roaming the streets, it brought hunters looking to bag a big game cat.

She had to admit to being intrigued by his unique condition. What trauma had he suffered that he punished himself in such a strange fashion?

Her door, which she'd left slightly ajar to hear her patient—and allowed the feline from hell to wake her—swung fully open as Jack wheeled himself in. He appeared ready to fight, his hair disheveled, his one good fist clenched.

"What's wrong?" he barked upon seeing her sitting amidst the blankets.

"Your cat tried to kill me." She stuck to the truth.

He glanced at the sleek menace who groomed herself on the dresser, acting all innocent. Harper wasn't fooled.

"Dorothy doesn't like people," Jack offered without apology.

"Then why did she come into my room?" Harper offered a sizzling glare which the cat deigned to ignore.

"Because Dorothy is under the impression she owns the house."

"Does she?"

The man had the nerve to shrug and say, "Maybe? I mean, she was here before me."

That made no sense. "She can't have been here that long. Unless she was a kitten." She squinted at Dorothy. "She seems awfully fit for her age."

"More like she hasn't aged. Glinda never said much about her, but given she never leaves, I'm assuming she's just as cursed as me."

"You could have warned me about your cat."

"She's not really mine. Dorothy kind of does her own thing."

"You mean like waking up your guests by digging in her claws?" Her chest stung from the needle-like pricks.

"It's not the worst thing she's done."

"Then why not get rid of her?"

"I'm not going to toss her out of her home just because she's ornery, like me."

Harper pursed her lips. "I can't promise the same."

"Good luck getting a hand on her. Dorothy is quick and tricky, especially when I'm making fish. Steals it right from the frying pan."

"She better not lay a paw on my food. I don't share very well." She scowled at the cat who'd curled up to bask in the sunbeams on top of the hair brush she'd left on the dresser. A power move if she ever saw one. "I might run out and pick up a spray bottle today."

"If you can leave..." His ominous reply.

"What's that supposed to mean?"

"You're assuming you haven't gotten stuck inside my curse."

Resorting to mind games to get her to leave. She countered with, "Are you a witch or a warlock?"

"Hardly."

"Then I'm sure I'll be fine." She'd make a point to go out today just to prove she had nothing to fear. "Other than an ancient young cat, anything else you want to warn me about?"

"Pretty sure the house is haunted."

"Of course you have ghosts. The poltergeist tossing stuff kind, or the weird lights and cold spots type?"

The corner of his mouth lifted. "What if I said both?"

"I'd call lion shit. I am on to you. Your first attempt to get rid of me failed so now you're resorting to inflicting anxiety."

"Just trying to warn you that this house isn't like most. It has a past and personality that can prove startling to the unwary."

"I'll be fine. I've been around the world, in all kinds of places, some of them much spookier than this." That forest in Europe had been nasty with its whispers. She'd almost wandered off the path, a deadly mistake for the unprepared in the wilderness.

"Then that would make you braver than me. I went from Mom's house to college to here. Never really got to go anywhere in that time."

"Did you want to travel?"

"Hadn't thought of it much because I had different goals in my early twenties."

"And now? If you could escape?"

"I'd travel the world and taste everything." He wheeled himself out of the room.

A glance at her clock showed five am, godawful early, but she doubted she could sleep. Harper grabbed her clothes for the day, eyeing the cat warily as it hopped down from the dresser and followed her out of the room. Harper started the shower and while it warmed, she popped her head into Jack's room to see him lying on the floor, doing sit-ups.

Midrise, he paused to address her, a sheen of sweat on his face. "What?"

"I'm taking a shower. Try to not fall down any stairs or break any more bones while I'm busy."

"Ha-ha. FYI, I'm not usually clumsy."

"Just dumb apparently. Who gets up on a roof in a storm?"

"Someone trying to save the ceiling in the third bedroom. I would have been fine if not for Dorothy."

"She tried to kill you?" Harper could easily believe it. She looked back toward the guest room to see the feline sitting in the doorway, watching her still.

"More like I overreacted just as the rain really came down." He grimaced. "So much for the adage that a cat is supposed to land on all four paws. Might have been true for Dorothy, but wasn't for me."

"You should have shifted on your way down for that to work."

"I can't. Part of the curse. Human only inside the

boundary. Lion on the outside." He shrugged.

"That Glinda really did a number on you," Harper stated with a shake of her head. She still wasn't convinced it wasn't entirely psychological, but now had to wonder if perhaps there might be some hypnosis in there providing a strong subconscious command. "Going for my shower. You'll stay out of trouble?"

"I will do my best, Nurse," he said with an exaggerated roll of his eyes.

"Once I'm done, you better wash up. Or else."

"Or else what?" he taunted.

"Do you really want to find out?"

Once more his lips twitched. "Maybe?"

"Don't make me fetch the thermometer," she threatened as she left him to bathe in the lovely bathroom. The hot water soothed, and she let it soak into her body, readying her muscles for the bracing she would do to bring big Jack downstairs. By the time she emerged, the cat had made itself scarce but Jack sat in his chair in the hall, clean clothes folded on his lap. Pocket knife on top of them.

Her brow arched as she asked, "Going to stab me?"

"If I wanted to kill you, I'd use my bare hands. More satisfying," was his dry riposte. "This is for adjusting my garments."

"You sure you want to be doing that on your own?"

"I'll be fine. But if it makes you feel better, I'll give an unmanly yodel if I fail, so you can complete my emasculation."

The sarcastic wit almost made her laugh. "We'll do breakfast after you dress. Something hot is preferred."

"Wait, is that a hint?"

"Was I being too subtle?" she asked sweetly.

"And if I say no?"

"Then you'll see what happens when I'm not fed." She shook her head. "It's not pretty."

"How is feeding you my problem?"

"I'm your guest."

"I asked you to leave."

"Yet here I am, so be a good host."

"How about you be a less demanding nurse?"

"It's not too late for me to recommend an enema."

Both his brows hit his hairline. "Okay, enough with the anal threats. You are not shoving fuck all in my ass."

"There are other ways of administering laxatives." She sauntered to her room to finish dressing and grinned at the slam of the bathroom door.

Naughty of her to threaten, but what did he expect with his ornery attitude? In better news, he was so busy being mad at her, he forgot to sulk about his situation. She found it amusing that he made their breakfast from sealed packaging and watched her like a hawk until she'd finished eating.

The pancakes with sausage were perfect. She wondered what he'd make for lunch.

"So what are your plans for today?" she asked as she cleaned up from breakfast.

"Same thing I do every day. Check my stocks. Make some money."

Which left plenty of time for her to run errands and look into his supposed curse.

"It's a touch early for me to go shopping for some stuff. Mind if I explore the house?" she queried.

"Why?"

"To look for the witch's stash of spell books of course."

Jack snorted. "I told you there's nothing."

"According to you. Could be you missed something. Maybe an ancient totem, or some kind of altar hidden in the basement."

"The basement doesn't have any hidden rooms." He sounded so certain.

"What about ancient symbols or pentagrams on the floor?" More than one paranormal show she'd watched made it seem common when dealing with a curse.

Once more he uttered a noise of disdain. "The only weird symbols are on the fence surrounding the place. They appear to form the boundary of my prison."

"Are you saying they act like one of those electric boundary things they have for dogs? It triggers a zap when you pass it?" She gave an exaggerated twitch and buzzing sound.

He grimaced. "Nice analogy and annoyingly accurate."

"If the fence is tied into your curse, then why not smash those pickets to break the chain?"

"As if I haven't tried. By the time I get halfway through demolishing them, the first ones have grown back."

"No way," she breathed. Was it wrong she wanted to see it to believe it? She stood and went to a window to stare at the innocuous white fence. "The pickets look new."

"They're not, but I am allowed to paint them." To her surprise, he wheeled to the back door. "Come on."

"You want to go for a spin in the garden?"

"Not really, but I can see you still doubt me so let's get it over with." He managed to open the door and maneuver outside while not crushing the cat that went streaking past.

As she noted him wheeling for the fence she did have to caution, "I wouldn't recommend shifting. You'll mess up your casts and if you heal wrong, we'll have to rebreak the bones and start over."

"I'm not going to put any broken parts past the boundary. But I am going to show you just how fucked up this curse is and maybe then you'll stop playing the skeptic."

"It's not skeptical to ask questions."

"It is when you make it obvious you think I'm a head case. Ready?" He paused his chair by the fence.

"Ready for what?"

He extended his hand over the pickets and it turned instantly into a paw. A paw with fur that stopped and turned to flesh right on the property line.

CHAPTER SIX

Harper's mouth rounded as his hand and wrist—the only parts past the fence—went furry while the rest of him remained human-looking. "What the ever-loving fuck?" The expletive slipped from her.

He pulled his arm back in, normal hand. Over the fence, paw.

He kicked off his shoe and did the same with his foot. Paw. Foot.

"That shouldn't be possible," she breathed. Partial shifts did happen, usually because there was a medical issue that made it so the person couldn't fully go animal or human. But this? This kind of precise change? Unheard of. It gave her the creeps. In fact, looking around the yard toward the strange fence posts, a shiver tried to wiggle its way up her spine.

"The world is a strange place," Jack murmured. "Still think it's in my head?"

"Anything is possible," was her prim reply, as she grabbed the handles to his chair and wheeled him back inside, away from the eerie feeling of the yard. "Has anyone else had difficulties? Any visitors that transformed upon leaving?"

He shook his head. "Nope. Just me. Although, I will note, I've not had many guests. I tend to discourage our kind from dropping in. I didn't want to inadvertently trap anyone."

"Your mother visits."

"Too often." Spoken with a glower.

"Oh how horrible, a mother who loves you. Trade you my dad. With him, you can expect missed birthdays, rare visits, and a basic lack of anything nurturing."

"Ouch."

"Let me tell you, it's not as great as you think."

"You don't talk to him?"

"Nope. And I have no interest."

"Surely—"

She cut him off. "We're not discussing my daddy issues. The reason I asked about your mother's visits, is because the fact she comes and goes without turning into a lion indicates your condition appears restricted to you alone. Did the previous occupant have that issue?"

He shook his head. "Glinda was a witch, not a shifter. She came and went as she pleased."

"Glinda? The witch?" She pursed her lips. "Oh

wow, I didn't make the connection before, but now I get it—Ha. Ha. Funny. Glinda the witch. Dorothy the cat, which is odd, but I guess Toto is a little masculine. I guess you're the scaredy lion. Just missing the tinman and the scarecrow. Oh, and the great wizard himself."

"What the fuck are you talking about?"

"Did you think I wouldn't notice the *Wizard of Oz* references? I'm not that gullible. But good on you. You almost got me."

His lips twisted. "I wish this were a joke."

That led to her frowning. "You have to admit it's more than a coincidence."

"Which no one ever noticed before you."

"And this is why we need to examine your affliction from a different angle. We'll start with why you think it's a curse cast by a witch."

"Because she said so."

"She said, 'I curse thee,' and what? *Poof,* done?"

His shoulders rolled. "I don't remember much once I saw her. Basically, I was like oh shit, bad idea, and then I woke up naked. Fucking thorns sticking in my ass. My dick practically frozen to the ground."

"How drunk were you?"

"Doesn't really matter anymore."

Meaning very. "So this woman cursed you but you don't know how she did it and so you've been stuck here ever since. Did Glinda ever say anything about the parameters of her spell?" Perhaps the power of suggestion bound him, making it seem like magic.

"If she did, I don't remember. It's been a long time." His lips turned down. "I've forgotten more than I remember at this point."

"Tell me about Glinda. You lived with her for about a year before she died. What was she like?"

"Kind but strict. She didn't like clutter. Even a plate from a snack had to be washed and dried right away or I got zapped. And the zaps stung harder the longer I avoided doing the chore." His lips twisted. "That I remember."

"So an evil witch then."

"Not exactly. More like one old enough to want things done her way with the power to back it up. But she was also nurturing. Like I told you yesterday, she was a MacGyver in the kitchen, give her a potato and she'd make it into a masterpiece. She taught me how to cook." He glanced off as if in memory. "She had a sharp sense of humor. And she was very smart. She taught me all I know about stocks and investing."

"You sound as if you admired your jailor."

"She was more like a strict teacher, the kind who pushes a student to their full potential, using sometimes harsh, but effective, methods."

"What did she tell you of herself?"

"Bits here and there. She hinted at a sad past. When she died and left me trapped, I tried but couldn't find anything about her online. By the time we met, she'd long retreated from the world. She was a recluse until I came around and she cursed me to become her companion."

"Your prank must have been pretty severe to warrant such punishment."

"Not at all," he replied with a sad shrug. "I just shifted into my lion and crept into her yard. I guess I could have scared her enough for a heart attack, but it's not like I set her house on fire or anything."

"Well, then the punishment seems harsh for such a harmless Halloween prank."

"Blame loneliness. She lost her lover in a war and never had any children. She had Dorothy, but a cat isn't a replacement for a person with whom to talk and interact."

"She turned you into a pet she could converse with." A blunt assessment.

"At first, yes." He lifted his shoulder. "But as you noted, by the time a year had passed, I'd gotten fond of her."

"And then she died, leaving you stuck." Harper gnawed the tip of her thumb. "I'll admit, I don't have experience with spells or curses, but what I do know indicates there's usually a way to break it." She hoped he didn't ask what made her an expert all of a sudden. She had a feeling he'd not be impressed by a recitation of The Brothers Grimm.

"Which died with her."

She shook her head. "I find that hard to believe.

She had to have learned her magic from somewhere. I doubt she did stuff off the top of her head."

"I told you I found no books."

"You said the basement was empty, what about the attic?"

"There is no attic."

"Impossible. All houses have one and this roof with its peak most likely has a big one."

His lips pursed. "I think I'd have noticed if I had an attic. Whoever built this place sealed the ceilings tight."

"You're kidding, right? I saw the hatch in the hall. Like smack dab between my bedroom door and the bathroom."

"No." He shook his head. "There is no attic." The conviction in his tone made her wonder if she'd not seen things right.

When he left her for his office to check on stocks, Harper headed back upstairs. Sure enough, she could see the rectangular hatch overhead with its dangling string and pull ring.

A yank and the ladder emerged, unfolding and allowing a solid path up. Before she could climb, she heard him bellow. "Who the fuck are you?"

Had opening the attic released a spirit in the house? Harper shook her head. She couldn't believe that one day here and she was already jumping to superstitious conclusions.

Then she heard a familiar voice. *Oh no.* She wasn't

sure if she was more concerned for Jack or for the uninvited guest as she hurried downstairs to find her very pregnant cousin body blocking Jack who'd gotten cornered.

"Darcy, what are you doing here?" she asked.

Her big-bellied cousin wore a bright yellow maternity smock over lime green pants, both offsetting her fire engine red hair. "I heard Arik banished you to the country and came to save you!"

"Hardly banished. Our king asked me to give Jack a hand." She sidled around the belly to try and provide a shield from the brunt of Jack's ire.

"You were supposed to be on vacation hanging out with me!" Darcy pouted. "We were supposed to get our nails done, and our hair. Plus, I am in dire need of a Brazilian. It's a jungle down there and I refuse to watch myself having a hairy walnut on the birthing video."

Harper kept a straight face, but poor Jack choked. "Sorry, Cuz, but I'm going to be busy with Jack for the next bit."

"So no mini putt with Dobbie and Dollie?" Darcy's other two kids. Cute but eternally sticky.

"Another time," Harper promised while crossing fingers behind her back. Darcy—as well as all her other cousins—had always been a little much for Harper to tolerate in large doses, but adding in all the loud and boisterous children made her even less eager for visits.

"You are coming to my shower, though, right?"

Saying no could be dangerous. "Uh, sure."

"The registry can be accessed via darcys-babyneedsdiapers dot com. Better hurry, there's only a few high-ticket items left." Darcy made no bones about her expectation.

Once more Harper lied. "I will be at your baby shower."

"Pinky swear." A sly Darcy held it out.

Uh-oh. Caught. Harper had no choice but link her finger and mutter, "I promise I won't miss your shower without a good reason." Maybe she'd find one between now and then.

"I really hope someone gets me the stroller for the shower." Darcy's less than subtle hint. "And I'm hungry. Who's feeding the baby?" She rubbed her tummy.

Harper glanced at Jack who scowled as he grumbled, "Can't have the baby starving. Get in the kitchen."

It was dumb to feel jealous as her cousin groaned her way through an epic sandwich. Then the man whipped up sweets in the form of chocolate cupcakes and a frosting so fluffy she died and went to heaven. By the time her cousin left with a box of treats, she almost liked Jack.

Until he opened his mouth.

"You're using me to avoid your cousin," he accused. "That's why you won't leave."

"Don't be silly. I love her. I would have totally

enjoyed hanging out every single second of the day with her and her kids." Thankfully her nose didn't grow with every false word.

"You are going to Hell for the epic lie alone." He shook his head. "Nice lady but she sounds exhausting."

"Right?" Harper blurted. "I mean, I love her, in small doses. I'm not the kind to be on the go all the time."

"But you travel."

"For work, I go. I take care of my patients. In my off time, I might explore a little. But I prefer to unwind somewhere quiet and beautiful."

"Must be nice to have that choice."

"Do you like being around a lot of people?"

His nose wrinkled. "I did a long time ago, but now I'm not sure if I could handle it."

"Is this a good time to warn you that being nice to Darcy—"

"I wasn't nice!" he interjected loudly.

"You fed her," Harper explained. "Which means she now thinks you're her friend."

"You exaggerate."

"She will be back. Probably with sticky offspring the next time."

He looked utterly horrified. "I'll lock the door."

"As if that will stop her," Harper scoffed.

"Tell your cousin no more visits!" he grumbled. "Now, I need to work."

"Excellent. I've got things to do."

"What will you be doing?"

"Exploring the attic. And before you say you don't have one, I've already pulled down the ladder, but Darcy arrived before I could explore."

"You found an attic?" His brows raised in surprise. "Where? Show me."

"It's on the second floor. Think you're up to climbing?"

"Try and keep up," he taunted, wheeling quickly to the steps.

He hopped more than half the steps without her aid, only agreeing to her support when he began to waver as his muscles tired.

Once they reached the landing, he collapsed onto his chair with a sigh before exclaiming, "Why do I see a ladder going into the ceiling?"

"The attic, duh. The whole reason we humped up the stairs."

He pointed. "What I mean is I see a ladder ending abruptly at the plaster, as in right through it, which doesn't seem right."

Harper stared at him then the ceiling. "I see a hole. About yay wide by this long." She held out her arms to show him. She then also played with the ladder, sliding it back up on its hinge, then down again. Once the door closed, he claimed to see only smooth, white plaster.

"You can't see the frame around the edges?" She lifted on tiptoe and reached but couldn't quite trace the outline for him.

"Nothing."

She squinted at the underside of the ladder stairs. "It's got some kind of a symbol etched into it."

That got his interest. "Does it look like a fleur-de-lys being stabbed by an arrow, like what's on the fence posts?"

"More like an eyeball with a cross through it."

"Possibly another spell," he muttered. "And I never suspected it was there." His head suddenly lifted. "Have you seen other symbols around the house?"

Her nose wrinkled. "Maybe? Could be I've seen them without seeing them, if you know what I mean." Kind of like the pile of junk on the counter that she kept meaning to put away only it kept growing. It didn't help she never stuck around long enough to care.

"I told you this house was tricky." He tapped his fingers on his leg. "What's up there?"

"I'm about to find out." She hauled down the ladder and climbed.

As her head, shoulders, and then upper body passed the threshold into the dark attic, he muttered, "And now you look like you've been sheared at the waist. Do you have any idea how disturbing it is to only see your legs sticking out of plaster? Fucking house!"

She couldn't even imagine how weird it must be from his perspective. The previous owner must have had a reason she didn't want him to see anything up here. Was this another example of hypnosis or an actual spell?

The darkness smothered the space and she had to dig out her phone to shine its flashlight. The bright glare bobbed over loose planks set over pink insulation packed between struts. Definitely not a secret witch lair. It appeared the attic was used for storage. The sight of a few boxes had her climbing the rest of the way in.

Jack yelled, "You, like, completely disappeared. Can you hear me?"

"Yeah. I'm in the attic with what looks like mostly junk." She read the label on a box. *Gerard's.* Inside, men's clothing of a long-forgotten style that included much polyester and wide collars on strangely patterned shirts. Another box labelled "shoes" held a few men's pairs as well as old ice skates, the kind that strapped on. Leaning against an angled rafter, yellowed pictures in heavy frames. A rocking horse that needed some paint to fix its faded and eerie face. An empty cradle.

What she didn't see? Any books. Point for her in proving that Glinda wasn't actually a witch. Unfortunately, it also left her without any tools that she could have tried using to nullify Jack's brainwashing or whatever it was blocking him.

She descended to find Jack waiting.

"Well?" he asked the moment she planted her feet.

"A bust. All junk unless you're into old kind of generic stuff."

"Yet she hid it from me." He stared in thought at

the ceiling. "And I never suspected. Which means perhaps the basement isn't as devoid as I thought. We should investigate it."

"Look at you, admitting you might not be right about everything, and faster than expected. I expected to prove you wrong at least another time or two before you asked me to help."

"I am not asking you for help."

"Oh? Then how do you plan to see the things you can't see? Hunh?"

His jaw tensed. "It's like you want me to use the garden shovel."

The threat curved her lips. "First you'd have to catch me." With that taunt, she spun from him and fled down the stairs.

"Of course, you'd strand me up here," he grumbled.

"Stop being so dramatic. Today's lesson on independence: coming down on your bum. Hold your injured leg in front of you, use your good leg to steady and brace, along with your hand."

"You can't be serious." His glare angled down the stairs to heat Harper.

She offered a cocky grin. "Or you can stay up there. It's up to you."

"And I see you're back to being annoying."

"Would you like a soother? You're whining again." Her hands planted on her hips.

"You're insufferable," he huffed as he slid out of his chair carefully and perched on the top step.

"I can't hear you! Why don't you get closer and repeat that?" She held a hand to her ear.

He humped down a step. "How is it none of your patients have killed you?"

"Because by the time they're capable, I leave."

"I am not defenseless," he argued, slipping down each stair faster now that he'd figured out how to balance.

"Yet just yesterday I found you living like a savage."

"A man's allowed to wallow."

"Not a real man. A real man, or woman for that matter, will look at the task daunting them and find a way to overcome it."

"If you start with motivational quotes I will run you over with my chair," he promised as he reached the last few steps. Rather than slide further, he braced his good foot on the floor, grabbed the railing, and heaved to his feet.

"You don't want me to tell you to take it one day at a time and that a smile is the best medicine?"

He groaned. "Why must you torture me?"

"What doesn't break you makes you stronger. Although in this case, the roof beat you but I'm sure you showed the ground who was boss. Oh wait, it broke you too. I'm sure there's something out there you can beat."

He flattened his lips in annoyance. His nostrils flared and she expected an explosion, only he suddenly relaxed and drawled, "I beat it every single morning."

The innuendo couldn't have been clearer. With some patients, she would have dumped something unpleasant in their lap. Others she would have slapped —and not been charged for it. Shifters handled conflict differently than humans. Insulted? A good whack could even that score.

But in this case, she could see he wanted her to be pissed. She used a different tactic with Jack. "Is that an invitation to watch?"

"No," he sputtered before wheeling away quickly.

Point for her. She'd won that round and for some reason, it left a grin on her face. It had been a long time since she'd had so much fun. What was it about Jack that brought out a lighter side? She was no-nonsense Nurse Ratched, not a flirty tease.

Then again, his fault for making it so much fun.

She found him in the kitchen in front of a door. He didn't look at her as he said, "The basement is through here."

"You going to lock me down there?"

"It's tempting, but you'd probably use a window to escape."

"Good point. The only way you're keeping me in one spot is by tying me hand and foot." She winked and wondered if he even thought of the fact his bed had four solid posters. He turned beet red and looked away.

Yup, it crossed his mind.

"You coming?" she asked.

"Why don't you see if there's anything there first?"

"M'kay." She headed down, the flick of a switch providing enough light to show a wide-open space. One corner held a massive furnace. Not far from it, a hot water tank. A washer and dryer took up another corner. Under the stairs, boxes neatly labelled. Electrical. Plumbing. Plaster/Paint. Everything tidy. The man liked to be organized.

A tour of the space proved to be a bust. The solid cinderblock construction appeared seamless and lacked any weird symbols. She even shoved her way behind the boxes under the stairs. Didn't find even so much as a single cobweb.

She trudged back up the stairs to find Jack at the stove, using a single crutch for support as he stirred a pot that smelled divine.

"Hot cider?" he queried.

"Trying to get me drunk?"

"Nonalcoholic. I don't drink. Haven't since that night."

"Really?" She couldn't help the surprised lilt. "I would have expected you to have spent a few in a drunken stupor of despair."

Laughter barked from him. "It wouldn't have helped. I got myself into this mess, I was determined to get out."

"How did you not give up?"

"Who says I haven't? It's been a while since I've tried anything. I think I've finally resigned myself to the fact I'm never leaving."

"I didn't take you for a quitter."

He arched a brow. "How long am I supposed to hold on to false hope?"

Would Harper have lasted even half as long as him?

Something must have shown in her expression because he growled, "Don't you dare pity me."

"I will if I want to. Your situation obviously sucks. But there has to be a way out."

"And you think that you'll find it in the few days you're here? Never mind the fact I've been here decades?"

"You seem to forget I know how men tend to search with their asses. Sometimes what you need is right in front of you, and you just can't see it."

"Okay smarty pants, did you find anything in the basement that I missed?"

"No."

Rather than be disappointed in her lack of discovery, he offered a smug, "Told you so." He turned off the stove and removed the pot, placing it on a trivet before sitting back down in his wheelchair. "Can you get the glasses?"

"Sure." Harper reached for the cupboard and opened it only to scream as grey fur sprang out. She reeled to escape and tripped over the wheel of his chair.

Jack yelled, "Bad kitty," while Harper flailed her arms and ultimately splatted.

In his lap.

To her surprise, he didn't shove her off.

To her other surprise, she didn't move either.

They stared at each other, a tingling awareness parting her lips. His nostrils flared and his expression softened. Their faces got close enough they could have kissed.

Which was when a dulcet voice chided, "Jackie, darling, unhand the nurse. What did we say about not doing anything that will get you sued for harassment?"

CHAPTER SEVEN

J ack couldn't decide if he should thank his mother's timing or lament the fact he needed to change the locks yet again. The woman did not understand boundaries. She trampled over his without care and most probably with intent.

She also had shit timing. Why did it have to be now? Jack found himself with a dilemma. He rather liked Harper in his lap. Her squirm to get herself free had his mind so deep in the gutter he had to hunch and hope his sweater hid any bulges.

He turned to the stove and offered an annoyed, "Mother. What are you doing here?"

"I came to help my darling baby of course. I thought for sure you'd have chased off your nurse by now." Mother eyed Harper head to toe. Most people cowed under that laser gaze, but not Harper. She not only met it, she perused right back.

He drawled, "I keep trying to convince her to leave, but Harper seems to think she can outstubborn me."

The contest broke as his mother cast him a sharp glance. "Don't tell me you've met your match."

"Hell, no!" He and Harper couldn't exclaim fast enough.

Harper cleared her throat. "You must be Mrs. Lantern. I'm Harper Jerome, your son's nurse."

"Jerome. I know that name," his mother mused, regarding Harper intently. "You look a bit like Dante Jerome, the opera singer, one of the few of our kind to make it to the big stage, and around the world at that. Are you related?"

Her lips pinched. "Yes. He's my father and a wastrel. We don't speak."

"How interesting," his mother murmured in reply.

Actually, it was. This Dante Jerome obviously hadn't been a great parent. For all his mother's faults, at least she'd always been present in his life.

He turned off the stove before the cider burned. "Well, Mother, as you can see, your rescue is unnecessary." This time at any rate.

When he'd first been trapped, he'd called for help, Glinda smirking as she offered him the use of her phone. His mother had arrived in a fury ready to kill. He'd expected to walk out of Glinda's house that same afternoon. Instead, his mother left, saying, "It's only for a year. It will be character building."

Only that year got extended, which finally led to

his mother doing everything in her power to help him break the spell. To no avail.

"I am glad to see you cooperating with treatment," his mother said, hovering over the pot and sniffing.

"Barely cooperating, but he's got the bitching down pat." Harper didn't lie.

Mother snorted. "Can't be that bad. You're still here."

"Only because the other option is being dragged around to do girly stuff with her cousin." He ratted her out.

Harper huffed, "Darcy is not that bad."

"You chose me and my charming personality over getting your nails and hair done with your cousin," he riposted.

"Did it ever occur to you I stay because of the food?"

His mother exclaimed, "He cooked for you?"

"Not really. I had to eat." He whisked his pot with more vigor than needed.

"What's for dinner?" his mother asked, fishing.

He cut her line. "Something from the freezer."

"Do the pasta with that rosé sauce first. It will dazzle her even though it's not fresh."

"I was thinking the chicken with the pesto rice." Mother's least favorite.

"I'll eat anything so long as it's not past its best before," Harper replied with a shrug.

"Once you taste really good food—freshly made being best—you'll see the difference," he insisted.

"If you say so."

He almost said, 'I'll show you.' Like, it almost slipped out with his mother's eagle eye watching. Instead, he gestured for a mug.

While Harper ladled the hot brew into it, his mother dove in with a new tactic. "So Harper, Arik told me you're a travel nurse. How fascinating, but surely you must get tired moving around all the time."

Harper shrugged. "One place is much the same as another. I'm there to do my job for however long it takes."

A reminder she would be leaving once Jack didn't need her.

"Ever thought of staying in one place? I know a local doctor—bear, not lion—very good at what he does. He's got a private clinic and is looking for someone to assist him."

"I guess it would depend on the salary. I get paid very well to coddle people like your son."

"Coddle?" he retorted. "You threatened to shove an enema in my ass if I didn't listen."

"And look at that, you behaved afterwards." Harper smiled and his heart skipped a beat.

"But my cheeks might never unclench."

Harper shook her head even as a hint of amusement still tilted her lips. To his surprise, his face stretched into a grin as well.

Mother uttered a small cough.

As if caught with her hand in the catnip jar, Harper turned serious. "About your son, Mrs.—"

"Don't you dare. My name is Sally."

Had his mother just given permission to use her first name? What was happening?

"Very well then, Sally. While I am aiding your son through this healing period, I am also investigating his affliction."

"Oh, I know nothing about broken bones, dear, other than that they hurt."

"She's not talking about my fractures, Mother," Jack explained. "Harper thinks she can waltz in like Sherlock Meow and figure out how to break my curse."

"Really? What a wonderful idea." His mother turned an assessing glance at Harper. "Fresh eyes might be just the thing. Luckily, I still have that file the detective compiled. I'll have it run over first thing."

A baffled Jack couldn't fathom how pleasant his mother was being with Harper. You could find his mother's image under the word "haughty" in the dictionary. She took pride in it, yet here she sat being not just helpful, but nearly *cheerful*.

Jack didn't trust or like it. He also had a bone to pick. "I thought I told you to burn that file. You said you had." At the time he'd been upset that yet another venue of hope had been shuttered.

"I said that to appease you. Just because you gave

up didn't mean I did." She turned to Harper. "What are you planning to try to help Jackie?"

"I'm not sure yet. I'd prefer to gather some more facts first. Especially since this is my first curse. I honestly didn't believe in curses until I met your son, and even now I'm not a hundred percent sure it's magic and not psychosomatic."

"You think he's doing this to himself?" Mother huffed.

"It's important to investigate all possibilities."

"In that case, you should convince him to have that séance I've been bugging him about. Madam Gizelle says if we contact the witch, she might give us the cure."

"We are not contacting dead people, Mother." He put a hand over his eyes.

"You know a fortune teller who can talk to ghosts?" Harper encouraged his mother.

"Oh yes, she's quite good. But she needs a conduit to them. Personal item, or in this case home."

"No," he stated firmly.

"Yes," Harper stated even more firmly.

He glared at her.

She arched a brow. "If you expect me to believe in magic and witches, then that means we explore every-thing, even talking to ghosts."

"It's most likely a charlatan." His mother had tried to get him to talk to a few over the first decade. All of them fake. Coming into his house and making knocking sounds, or telling him generic messages like, *someone on the other side is proud of all you've accomplished. I see them holding up a fork. Did you used to cook for them?* Not a stretch, considering his mother always made him prep homemade snacks for her guests.

"Madame Gizelle is the real deal," his mother promised. "She comes from Europe." As if that legitimized her claim.

Harper smiled wide. "I cannot wait to see this."

Mother clapped her hands. "I will speak to her at once about coming. Is tonight too soon?"

"I said no," Jack said. No one paid him any mind.

"Ignore him, he's just cranky I made him wash his balls."

Mother coughed suddenly.

Jack growled.

Harper smiled serenely. "Let's talk about this further once I settle Mr. Grumpiness down."

"I am not grumpy!" he growled.

"Tired? You've had a busy day. Want me to tuck you in for a nap?"

"We are not having a séance!" he shouted.

"Ignore him. He's probably running a fever. Don't worry, Jackie," Harper said, using his mother's nickname and making him grit his teeth. "I'll fetch my rectal thermometer the moment I see your mother out."

"Oh, I'm fine, dear. You take care of my Jackie. He's got a delicate constitution."

"I do not!" he muttered, even as no one paid him any mind.

Only when the door clicked shut did he explode. "Why would you do that?"

"Do what?"

"Encourage my mother to hold a sham in my home."

She blinked at him not so innocently. "I thought you said you tried everything."

"Everything that made sense. But having charlatans who pretend to speak to spirits, that goes too far!" He flung his good hand to punctuate.

"Wait, so you believe in a curse that keeps you bound to this property, but not a woman who can communicate with the dead? That makes no sense. You're the one who told me this place was haunted."

"It is. And I don't believe we should be bothering them."

Her mouth rounded. "You're afraid of making the ghosts mad."

"I'm stuck here. The last thing I need is to be living some poltergeist horror movie on a daily basis."

A slight dimple dented her cheek. "What if I promised to bring a gallon of holy water?"

"That only works on vampires."

"We could burn spirit-repelling incense?"

"As if my mother didn't make me gag on the smoke for months as she tried various concoctions."

She tapped her lower lip. "I wonder if she kept a

list of the kinds she tried. There can be health benefits with an aromatherapy approach. I assume she brought in priests, shamans, and other witchy type people to see if they could do anything."

His lips turned down. "In the beginning, I wanted to believe I could escape. But the curse was too strong."

"There has to be a way to break it," she uttered with confidence.

"I thought you didn't believe in this stuff."

"I don't, or should I say didn't, but now having met you, I'm curious to see if I can be proven wrong."

"To my possible detriment," he grumbled.

"Ah yes, because the status quo is so much better."

He scowled. Something he did too much. He also hated that she made some sense. Was he so worried about upsetting the balance of his boring life that he wouldn't try something new?

"Fine. You want to have a séance? We'll have a séance. But if shit goes to haunted hell, you're not leaving until you fix it."

"Why Jackie, darling," she teased. "Is this your way of asking me to stay?"

Must be something wrong with him because a part of him almost said, *Would you?*

CHAPTER EIGHT

With Jack sulking in his office about the upcoming event with the seer, Harper did the one thing she'd been putting off all day.

She went to the little gate in the picket fence and walked through it. She emerged on the other side—wearing clothes, not fur—and blew out a breath of relief. The supposed curse still only affected Jack. A glance back at the house made her wonder if she should go back in. At the same time... A lack of chocolate other than the kind for baking led her to walk quickly down the street. Surely he could handle himself for twenty minutes?

She entered the variety store, the bell overhead ringing. As she shopped, she caught pieces of conversations from the other patrons.

"...ripped me off because my car is still making that weird noise."

"...and then she had the nerve to tell me my kid was the bully not hers. So I gave her a smack and told her if she insulted..."

"Apparently there's a cripple living in that house with the short fence. Joey says his dad was saying how he gets stuff delivered all the time. Like expensive shit," a male voice loudly whispered.

"Think he's got one of those new game systems?" a nasally boy replied.

"Don't matter if he does. We can always pawn the shit we take and buy one."

It occurred to her that the miscreants probably spoke about Jack. She could have confronted them then and there, however, past experience had shown they might cower in the moment while she harangued them for their poor life choices, but once she was out of sight they'd simply return to their bad habits. They needed a proper lesson.

They finished their conversation with an actual plan to break in and even conveniently set an approximate time. She set an alarm in her phone for the time stated, and then headed for the checkout lane. Suddenly leaving Jack alone didn't seem prudent. He might think himself tough, but reality had him at a huge disadvantage.

Her bag of candy swung as she hurried back to the house, walking into the smells of heaven—also known as dinner. Not leftovers after all. A pasta with white creamy sauce, chunks of salty meat, and cheese. The light garlic toast perfectly complemented.

It smelled so heavenly she decided that she could break the news to Jack about the potential burglars after they ate. No reason to spoil a good meal listening to him freak out when they still had plenty of time before their arrival.

She couldn't help but notice how Jack kept staring at her as she ate. She tried to keep quiet, but the food! She just couldn't.

"You are the best I've ever had," she sighed, leaning back in her chair.

"Uh, excuse me?"

She patted her belly. "That was incredible. If I had more room, I'd be begging for more."

"You like to eat." Stated not asked.

"Good food makes my mouth sing. What's not to like?"

"Some people are just about fueling their bodies."

"Doesn't mean it can't taste delicious." She set down her glass of watermelon-infused water to eye him across the table. "You must agree, or you wouldn't go through the trouble."

"It's always been a pleasure of mine. Although, I didn't actually start taking it seriously until a decade ago. Being stuck here, I didn't have much to enjoy, so I had to find things that made me happy."

"I just need books."

"You read?"

She nodded. "I used to always have a paperback with me, but now," she patted the phone in her pocket, "with ebooks, I'm never bored."

"I still prefer the feel of a real book," he admitted.

With him relaxed, she finally revealed what she'd overheard. "So I think some young men are going to try and rob you tonight."

"What?" He spewed a mouthful of his water in shock.

She waved a hand. "I overheard them at the store. Something about you being old and fragile."

"I'll show them," he growled.

"You'll do nothing. You're still broken, and we don't want to be messing with your recovery."

"I am not letting them rob me."

"They won't. I'll handle it."

"You?"

She flashed teeth at him. "Ever heard the expression 'scared straight?'"

"You really think a lion attacking them is going to make them turn from a life of crime?" He shook his head. "More like they'll run and tell people I have a giant pet cat which will lead to them watching me more closely, making it harder for me to escape the nights I do need to stretch my legs."

"So what do you suggest?"

"If you're going to scare them, do it right."

"I take it you have an idea."

"This wouldn't be the first time I was harassed."

His grin looked positively mischievous, a change from the dour man that did something to her chest. He really was quite handsome.

And devious.

By the time he'd outlined the plan, she was almost applauding. This would be quite entertaining, and it didn't require too much preparation.

The most annoying part? They had to wait. The boys had said 11:00 p.m. By 11:20 she thought maybe she'd misunderstood, until she heard the scuff of a foot by the back door.

Jack had predicted this given the deadbolt on the front would baffle all but the most adept at lockpicking. They'd left the back entrance unlatched lest the miscreants break a window.

The knob turned and the door swung open, hiding her behind it. The boys entered, scuffing their feet and breathing hard, then whispering even more huffily.

"Where should we start?" Asked by one smelling intensely of BO.

The taller of the boys glanced around. "We should start with his living room."

As they both headed for the swinging door, she slammed the back door shut and ducked out of sight.

"What's that? Who's there?" BO turned with wide eyes.

"Just the wind, you pussy."

"Can't we turn on a light?" whined BO.

"Don't be fucking stupid. We don't wanna be

seen," Tall Boy scoffed, never mind the fact he didn't have a single quiet bone in his body.

"Okay." BO kept glancing suspiciously behind as he followed the leader into the hall.

Harper crept quietly behind them, entering the hall as they turned into the living room.

"I see a tv," announced BO. "And is that a gaming console in the corner?"

Harper flattened by the door and waited.

It took a few seconds before Tall Boy said, "What's that smell?"

Followed by a shriek. "It's the headless horseman."

As they rushed to get away from Jack waving a pumpkin head that glowed in the dark, they never thought to pay attention and missed the leg Harper stuck out to trip them. They hit the floor in a tangle of legs while Jack neared with the floating pumpkin head. Only when the glow provided enough illumination did she crouch down and utter a gargling, "Brains. Brains."

The shriek BO uttered almost shattered glass. He launched himself from Tall Boy and slammed into the front door, pounding on it and screaming before managing to find the locks. He fled, screaming, while Tall Boy, blubbered, "Wait for me."

As Harper closed the door behind them, she turned and leaned against it. Jack had the pumpkin head in his lap, lighting up his diabolical smile. "Well?"

She couldn't help but laugh. "That was rather

satisfying. But do you think it will straighten them out?"

"Who cares? That was fun." His amusement shaved off years of cynicism.

"I haven't put on a costume since I was a kid," she stated, eyeing her zombie makeup in the mirror.

"I don't dress up for Halloween, but I do give out stuff to those brave enough to show."

"I thought you were worried about the curse."

"With shifters. Not the human kids that come trick-or-treating."

"Explains why you had a jack-o-lantern handy. It's late now. We should get you up those stairs."

He grimaced. "I am going to end up with a mega thigh before the other one heals."

"It won't be that bad. If you're healing as expected, you'll be able to start putting weight on that heel soon."

"Ah yes, the stumping around phase."

"I hear a violin," she chirped as she tucked under his arm to give him support.

"You have a terrible bedside manner."

"Not true. If you were truly sick in bed, you'd think I gave you top notch care. But you can walk and talk, as evidenced by the bitching. You're just using your slow ungainliness to be lazy."

"Lazy?"

"You have another word for the state I found you in?"

"I wasn't that bad."

"You reeked."

"And now?"

As if his query forced her, she did sniff, the scent of the soap he'd used, mixed with a musk all his own. He smelled good enough to eat. "You're not rancid."

He chuckled. "Guess I won't have an ego problem with you around."

She let him use the washroom first, turning down his sheets for him, noticing how he'd made an attempt to make his bed. A bed that didn't smell pleasant.

By the time he entered, she'd stripped it and was hunting for fresh bedding.

"Linen closet in the hall," he offered rather than argue.

She had him park and hold a corner while she went across and did the tug and heave to put the fitted sheet in place. A fresh comforter was spread across the top. He tossed the pillow with its clean covering at her. She caught it and placed it at the head of the bed.

"You good for the night?" she asked.

He nodded. "See you in the morning."

"Holler if you need me." She went to leave only to hear a grunt. She turned to see him standing on his one good leg, wincing. Immediately, she flew to his side. "What did you do?"

"Whacked my bad arm," he growled. "I'm fine."

"Shut up and let me help you into bed." She went to lean past him to push the chair, but he caught her arm and drew her gaze.

"I said I'm fine."

She yanked her arm free and arched a brow. "Are you?" She shoved him in the chest, forcing him to fall on the bed, but he didn't go alone.

His good hand shot out and grabbed her, dragging her down atop him.

She landed on his chest, half-splayed, her face mere inches from his.

Their gaze locked.

Nothing was said. Words would have broken the yearning stretching between them.

She couldn't have said whose head moved first.

Hers.

His.

Didn't matter.

Their lips touched and her senses exploded. Her heart began to pound. Her body pulsed.

Ached.

She retained enough wits to know she shouldn't be kissing her patient.

She pulled back, and uttered a breathless, "Night," before fleeing. However, closing her eyes and forcing herself to sleep didn't let her escape the fact she liked Jack a lot more than she should.

CHAPTER NINE

W hat just happened?

Jack had kissed his nurse.

Bad idea. Mostly because it felt so good.

For a moment, as their lips melded, a simple embrace almost turned into something more. He'd wanted to intimately connect with someone.

With her...

A good thing she'd had the sense to halt things because he'd certainly not had the will to do so. Had things gone further there would have been so much regret to unpack in the morning.

Not about the sex, though. That would have been epic. For his part, he couldn't deny his attraction to her. And no, it wasn't just because he couldn't get out and meet people, or because the women he met online turned out to be duds. It was just that he knew what to expect when they entered his house for a hookup—

including the fact they'd leave before morning. None of those were ever serious, though, mostly because of him. He couldn't stand having people around him for long. They quickly got on his nerves, which was why sleeping with his nurse would be a bad idea.

Oddly enough, he didn't yet have a problem with Harper. Through some kind of miracle, he actually could tolerate having her around. Unlike his first care-takers, Harper demanded independence from him. Didn't hover and let him know she wasn't there to be his maid or be at his beck and call. She was crazy stubborn and bossy, but also wickedly intelligent. Couldn't pull a fast one over her. If he slept with her and then she left because of it, Arik or his mother would probably send someone new to try and wipe his ass.

Add in the fact they didn't even like each other and the reasons why they shouldn't get involved outnumbered the reasons they should.

A good thing Harper never even suggested it. The first nurse had offered, and he'd snapped, *"I'd rather lick my own arse than have you near it!"*

He fell asleep thinking of Harper and woke in the wee hours, unsure of what he'd heard. Had the thieves returned? The cat tried to kill Harper again? The feline had a vicious streak and more than once he'd almost tossed it from the property only to relent at the sight of the furry face with those big eyes.

Rather than struggle into the chair and roll himself to see, he listened. Could be the house creaked overly loud. Or the cat caused trouble again. He'd learned not to leave breakables anywhere close to edges. He and Dorothy maintained a casual relationship. He didn't bother her. She didn't try and eat his face when he slept. What he'd yet to figure out? Where she shit and ate. He'd never found a litter box in the house, nor had Glinda ever fed the cat. He'd asked her once about it, and she'd shrugged. "Dorothy takes care of herself."

Mostly. The hair she shed all over the place begged to differ.

Nothing marred the serenity of night and yet he didn't fall back asleep, or did he?

A sudden whispered, "Did you hear that?" almost had him screaming. A glance at the foot of his bed showed Harper standing there in a two-piece pajama set, the shirt loose but molding her figure enough he could see the outline of her breasts, unfettered by a bra. Stealthy and sexy. Talk about utter torture.

"Hear what?"

"I'm thinking those idiots came back." She whirled, ready to fight.

"Most likely the house settling. She's noisy but solid."

Harper snorted. "I hear a sneeze. Thought it might be you."

"Not me."

"I'll go check the main floor." She left without even waiting for him.

It left him eyeing his chair. Stupid broken leg. He

still couldn't believe he'd fallen from the roof. The timing had been so bad. He'd been up by the chimney, hammering down some flashing that got loose, when he'd sat on his haunches to eye his work. Which was when Dorothy suddenly leapt to the lip of the chimney, scaring the piss out of him.

He'd recoiled slightly in surprise, his balance slightly off, but controlled, and then the deluge hit. The rain came down in a torrent that blinded and pummeled. Dorothy yowled before streaking past, just a slight nudge and then he toppled, swept by the current sluicing from the roof.

Launched into the air, he had a brief second where he knew this was gonna hurt.

It did. Hurt enough he'd actually called him mom.

The memory swing helped occupy his mind as he used one braced hand and a foot to slip himself into the chair. Then he scooted to the hall, knowing Harper had already reached the bottom of the stairs. He caught sight of her backside before she went down the hall to the kitchen.

No screaming—or snarling—occurred, but that didn't stop him from slipping onto the stairs and humping his way down on his ass quickly, which meant jarringly. *Ow. Ow. Ow.* Not said aloud. He wasn't about to further emasculate himself.

At least his wheelchair remained parked at the bottom of the stairs. A pause at the main floor netted him the murmur of voices, the cadence familiar. He lost his tension. Only one person would dare show at this time of the night. With less haste, he got into his chair and wheeled himself to the kitchen, which was brightly lit and smelling of coffee. It almost penetrated his dark mood. But then he eyed his mother sitting at the table, having a chat with Harper.

"What the fuck, Mother?"

"Is that any way to speak to me?" Mother huffed.

"I will speak to you any fucking way I like at 4 a.m.," he snapped. "We talked about this. You can't just come over any time of the day. You're costing me a fortune in locks."

His mother sniffed. "I don't know why you bother. We both know there's isn't a lock in the world that can keep me from you, Jackie."

"At least your mother cares," Harper muttered. "Some of us would have killed for that growing up."

The tidbit she revealed didn't ease his annoyance with his mother. "I don't want you skulking around the house—especially at four-o-fucking clock in the morning. You should have called."

"We both know your phone is on sleep mode until seven am."

"There's a neat modern invention called voicemail, you know," his sarcastic reply.

"Which you tend to ignore."

"For fucks sake, then text me. You know I check those and email while drinking my morning coffee."

"This is important. It couldn't wait."

"I doubt it," his dark retort.

Harper chimed in. "Actually, you should listen to what she has to say. It appears the miscreants we frightened off last night got a little drunk, and around 3 a.m. thought it was a good idea to try and report zombies were coming from your house to take over the world."

"They went to the cops?" Jack asked incredulously.

Mother nodded. "Luckily, the officer on duty is a tiger I know. He handled the thieves and sent them off with a warning about wasting police department time with frivolous claims and let me know about it. Hence why I came over to ensure you were fine. The nerve of those boys, breaking in while you're defenseless. I should call Terrence back and demand he throw them in jail."

Jack sighed as he rolled to the fridge. "I'm not defenseless, Mother."

"Indeed, you aren't. A good thing you had Harper to defend you."

Said defender choked while Jack scowled into his fridge and began pulling out bacon and the fixings for a breakfast sandwich for what promised to be a long day.

His mother kept talking. "I've tried to convince Jackie to have an alarm system installed, but my sweet boy is convinced he's invincible."

"I'm home like ninety-nine point nine percent of the time. Why would I waste my money?"

"You keep changing the locks," his mother pointed out. "That's expensive too."

"I don't like the idea of cameras watching me. And those motion alarms and shit are noisy as fuck. Bad enough the smoke alarm battery always goes dead at 2 a.m."

"You see what I'm dealing with," his mother complained. "I try to protect him, and he just won't listen."

Harper commiserated. "He's a man. They're stubborn that way."

"That's sexist," he retorted as he lit the burner on his stove.

"Not if it's true," was Harper's quick riposte.

"Do you really want to irritate the man about to make your food?"

"Would you really be so petty as to ruin it on purpose just to punish me? The joke's on you. I'm fine with ordering takeout," Harper challenged right back, and he couldn't help a small chuckle that he tried to hide.

His mother thankfully remained oblivious. "You'll be glad to know Madame Gizelle has agreed to join us this evening to conduct the séance."

He groaned. "Must we?"

"Why not?" Harper queried. "After all, it's not like you're going anywhere or have pressing plans."

"Maybe I wanted to wash my hair. Or catch a movie on the television. There's a Halloween marathon playing."

"Don't be a pussy." Harper gave no quarter.

"I am not scared," he huffed, flipping the sizzling bacon.

"Meaning we're back to the whining. I thought we'd gotten past that."

"It is not whining. I don't want to do it!" He waved his spatula.

"Too bad. So sad. It's happening. Which means you should probably prepare some finger foods for after."

He shot her a glare over his shoulder. "You seriously expect me to make canapes for this joke?"

Harper nodded seriously. "I do."

Damned if he didn't want to laugh again. He certainly fought a smile as he noted the sparkle in her eyes.

Mother just had to chime in. "Ooh, you should do those lovely little pastry things with the meat and cheese. And those fig bites with the prosciutto and cheese."

"Ooh, that sounds delicious." Harper licked her lips lightly. Just the tip of her tongue and he went instantly hard.

Fuck me.

He concentrated on making breakfast while Harper and his mom discussed finger foods. At the same time, he mentally catalogued what he had to cook with because, damn it, he would create some amazing canapes for Harper. The way she rolled her eyes when she ate her breakfast sandwich had him eager to have her looking orgasmic again.

With food. Although, he did have to wonder if she'd make the same kind of beautiful face and noises during sex.

Not that he'd find out, mostly because his mother stuck around after breakfast, cock blocking him from making a bad decision. He shouldn't be even thinking of fucking his nurse. To that end, he did his best to avoid her as she and his mother rearranged his dining room to be séance friendly, whatever that meant. The numbers on his screens scrolled, and he reclined in his chair in front of a window and napped.

He emerged to make lunch: grilled cheese—three different kinds—with tomato bisque soup—made from scratch because he hated canned stuff. Harper had two servings and squirmed in happiness a few times.

How had he ever thought her dour? She was a woman who knew what she enjoyed. She worked hard. She took pleasure in tasting.

I'll give her something to make her mouth explode with happiness. His cock sulked when he chose to go with real whipped cream instead of a salty filling.

He spent the afternoon rolling out pastry dough—a challenge, given his one-handedness—cutting it into shapes, and placing them in layers separated by savory fillings. He wore headphones to avoid listening to his mother and Harper getting along. A rarity. His very strong-willed mother tended to scare people off. She had few friends and had never actually married. His dad hadn't even stuck around for the pregnancy. He couldn't recall her actually dating. And she had strong opinions on the woman—*"Hussies after your money."*—he'd seen from time to time.

To his bafflement, his mother appeared to be getting along with Harper. The two of them chatted like old friends, his nurse the most at ease he'd seen her yet. Should he take it as a warning sign?

He prepared a simple dinner of mushroom risotto, smoked ham and gouda cheese stuffed chicken breasts seasoned and butter fried to perfection, along with parmesan roasted green beans.

Harper devoured and exclaimed while his mother beamed. It suddenly occurred to him something was afoot. Mother launched the attack, following him when he went to fetch dessert—creampuffs with different fillings and drizzles.

His mother sidled close as he plated to say, "I approve."

"Excuse me?" He didn't glance at her as he grabbed a second plate, not happy with how the first turned out. He handed the failure to his mother and started again.

"I can see how much you want to impress her."

"Don't know what you're talking about," he riposted, trickling some icing sugar over the cream puffs. Sparkles would have been better. He didn't make desserts often.

"Oh, come on, Jackie. It's so obvious you're trying to lure Harper with your fine cooking skills. A brilliant plan. She does love her food. And you like to make it. It's a perfect match."

He almost choked despite his mouth being empty. "Not happening, Mother."

"Why not? I can see you like her and it's obvious why. She's intelligent. Beautiful. Not wishy washy or a pushover. Why do you think I approve?"

"Be quiet before she hears you!" He shook his spoon at her.

"She's gone to the washroom. It's fine. So speak the truth. You like her."

"Harper is here to work."

"And?"

"I'm her patient. It's not ethical."

"Fate doesn't care about ethics."

He whirled in his chair to narrow his gaze on his mother. "What does fate have to do with anything?"

"Just look at the perfect storm of events that led to you being together. Harper is rarely in between jobs. And even more rarely available for a few weeks. You're never clumsy. And yet you somehow managed to injure yourself bad enough you needed help at home."

"None of that is fate."

"Fine, then how about compatibility?" His mother didn't let up. "I've seen the two of you together. How animated you are when you talk."

"You mean argue."

"Bah, it's lively chatter. It's obvious you enjoy each other's company."

Was it? He'd have to scowl more. "She's only here temporarily."

"But that could change with the right incentive," Mother cajoled. "Do you know Harper's never been married?"

"And?"

"One of her reasons is because she has no interest in having children."

Like him. He'd never been the kind to understand it. Years of being locked away hadn't changed that. "I get the impression she's not into relationships." She'd dropped enough hints about her dad to let him know she had trust issues.

"Bah. I'm sure you could charm her into changing her mind."

"I am not dating my nurse, Mother."

And that was final.

But damned if the idea hadn't been planted, and when Harper almost orgasmed having dessert, he couldn't help but stare, wondering what it would be like to be married or even involved with someone like her. How much would it hurt when she left? Because she would. She, a person who traveled the world, would never want to be bound to one place.

It would never work. Not while he remained cursed.

The doorbell rang at precisely 8 p.m. The séance

itself would be later as Madame wanted to set up prior —a.k.a. plant her tricks to fake it. Whatever. Despite the weirdness in his life, and his belief in ghosts, Jack didn't think Glinda lingered. The presences he'd encountered hadn't felt familiar, meaning the medium would be wasting her time. If she wasn't a charlatan like the rest who'd come by, claiming they could talk to ghosts.

His doubts only increased once he met Madame Gizelle of the fluffy, multicolored hair and earrings so big they hit her shoulders.

The woman shook long nails of bright yellow at him. "Look at you with the cage around your aura. Human in. Lion out. Lovely spellwork."

He could have rolled his eyes. As if he'd not heard that before. "Can you remove the cage?"

She pursed her rouged lips. "Doubtful. Not my kind of magic."

A convenient reply.

"I'll be in my office. Call me when it's time." He wheeled away and just as he went to close the door, Dorothy streaked in.

More surprising, the sudden appearance of Harper less than ten minutes later. She slipped into his office and eased the door shut.

"Hiding too?" he taunted.

"Not exactly. More like here to give you a warning. Darcy's back."

"Your cousin?" He pursed his lips. "Why?"

"So I might have slipped up when she called me and mentioned I couldn't go to the movies because we were doing something with your mother and she got the wrong idea and came over."

"Wrong idea about what?"

Harper grimaced. "That you and I... that is we... let's just say she thought she needed to come over."

"Tell her to leave."

"I did. But she's insisting on staying for the séance as is my other cousin who came with her."

He blinked. "Wait, are you saying she brought a stranger?"

"Not exactly a stranger. Jexy is another cousin."

"I don't know this person, nor do I want to," he growled. "Get them out or I'm cancelling the whole thing."

"Don't be such a drama llama. It's not a big deal. Not to mention, when your mother met them, she insisted they stay and bragged about your after-séance snacks."

He sighed and rolled his head back. "This is a nightmare."

"It will only be for a few hours."

"Forever," he moaned. "And for what? We all know it's going to be fake." Caged aura indeed.

Harper's expression turned pensive. "I was watching. She didn't install anything."

"While you were there. But you left her alone. She's probably got the room wired by now."

"And if she does, I'll find it. You seem to forget, I'm a girl of science. I'll look for that before turning to the supernatural."

"How long until the ordeal starts?"

Her lips twitched. "Not long. Madame Gizelle was waiting for some kind of planetary alignment."

"And it's comments like that which make me want to walk away."

"Think of it as an immersive theatric episode."

"I hate you," he grumbled as she wheeled him out of his office to the dining room.

"I know. Let that keep you warm when the chilly ghosts pay us a visit."

"Yes, Nurse Harpy," he muttered.

And did she get mad? No. She cackled. "Do you know how often I've heard that? I've also heard Lady Harpy. Evil Harpy. And my favorite, Harpy Cunt."

Contrition hit. "I wasn't trying to insult you." Only he had.

She put a hand on his shoulder. "I'm not so fragile that I can't handle banter. Even the less than flattering kind."

"Won't happen again," he swore.

"No, don't say that because we both know you will, and I will continue to play the violin when you whine."

"I don't whine," he said with a sulk.

"You were just doing it in your office."

His lips twisted. "You can't tell me you think this will accomplish anything."

"You want me to believe in witches and curses, so how is this any different? I think we should go in with an open mind." Just as she moved forward, she added in a low whisper, "And bust any signs of cameras or speakers."

It put a smile on his face as they entered his dining room lit up by candles, one in each corner plus a fifth in the middle of his table. Right on the wood.

Would it have killed them to slip something under it?

Harper parked him at the head of the table. As warned, Darcy had returned with Jexy, a thick woman with teased black hair and bright lipstick. All shifters. Even Madame the psychic. Lions for them all but this Gizelle.

He eyed the psychic where she sat across from him, her eyes closed, hands flat on the table. Feline, but not lion. He'd wager tiger.Darcy kept glancing past everyone to the kitchen. Had she spotted the platters of hors d'oeuvres? He'd better make sure Harper tried one of each before Darcy tried to take them home in her giant purse from which he'd have sworn he saw the corner of a plastic container peeking. She'd come prepared.

After a bit of seat shuffling and chatter that Jack tuned out, Madame Gizelle spoke. "Silence."

The room quieted.

He didn't know what to expect. Some of the others had started with a prayer of sorts, an incantation, a plea for spirits to visit. One even rolled up her eyes while pretending to be a ghost speaking by using a deeper voice.

This psychic said not one word. Made not a single motion.

The first sign of anything began with a cold breeze, the kind to cut through clothes and chill the skin. It swept past him and circled the candle on the table, making it flicker and sputter.

Madame Gizelle stared at the flame until it steadied, bigger than before, and with an intense blue center. Her expression tightened and the flame grew, stretching and growing, undulating as it rose.

Not a single murmur escaped as they all stared at the strange antics of the flame which grew limbs and defined features.

Only he recognized the final shape.

The name whispered from his surprised lips. "Glinda."

CHAPTER TEN

A ghost appeared above the candle and Harper gaped.

Before the séance began, Harper had waffled between skeptical and wanting something to happen. This in contrast to Jack who remained convinced the whole thing was a joke. It didn't help they'd somehow ended up with an audience, Darcy and Jexy flying to rescue their favorite cuz.

Supposedly.

It didn't escape Harper that Jexy eyed the house and Jack a little too avidly. Hold on a second. Hadn't Jexy just divorced her third husband?

The recollection led to her staring at her cousin who'd taken the spot on Jack's left. When her cousin stubbornly didn't move at Harper's approach, she offered a sweetly spoken, "How is that rash on your ass doing? Did that cream I prescribed you work? It's usually really good with fungal infections."

Jexy's jaw dropped.

In that rare silence, Harper added, "And what about—"

Before she could finish the sentence, Jexy slid over to the empty seat. Harper plopped beside Jack, who rolled his eyes heavenward while his mother smirked and Darcy. Uh-oh. Darcy looked contemplative. Never a good sign.

Madame Gizelle remained in her Zen-ish pose as they settled down and waited for something to happen. The candles in the room burned bright and steady, making the sudden draft very noticeable. It tickled by Harper's cheek as it passed between her and Jack. The candle on the table sputtered and danced violently, the flame flicking left and right, tall and short, before expanding.

It literally widened and extended in height, a thing of twisted oranges and reds, yellows too, but at the very core of it a blue, and that blue took a recognizable shape. A woman framed in a dress a style no longer in common use with a tight waist, flared skirt just past the knees, a trim bodice, and tight sleeves. Hair swept into a chignon. The face held an angular perfection that showcased sharp cheekbones, a fey chin, an aquiline nose, and the most piercing green eyes.

A stranger to Harper, but Jack whispered, "Glinda."

This was the old witch who kept him prisoner? She'd expected a hag.

As if hearing her thought, Glinda pivoted, her flame shrouded, body snapping and crackling. Her head canted. "Yes, I was quite beautiful in my prime." She smiled as she lifted her chin, her voice a shivery whisper. "Back then, I didn't need powers to get what I wanted."

Harper stared and tried to find the source of the hologram. She saw no projector, no strings, nothing to explain the flame woman.

Jack muttered, "Nice trick. Not buying it, though."

Gizelle remained silent and focused, staring ahead without blinking at the fire-rimmed shape.

The ghost leaned forward, bending unnaturally that she might bring her face close to Jack's and offer a throaty chuckle as she said, "My pretty kitty is all grown up."

The phrase caused him to flinch into a rigid pose before his gaze met Glinda's. "How do I know it's you?"

"You dropped the eggs the first time you cooked. All twelve on the floor. Such a mess and then you made it worse smearing it all around."

His lips flattened.

Glinda undulated, her feet attached to the flame despite her leaning towards Jack. "The day I left I was getting a lamb rack because you wanted to try your hand at roasting one with pistachios and cherries."

"You didn't come back."

"Because I died." Glinda's dry reply.

"I know. You left me stuck." His lower lip jutted, and Harper couldn't blame him.

"That was unfortunate." Glinda shrugged.

"Unfortunate?" he squeaked. "It's been more than twenty bloody years."

"That long? Seems like only yesterday." Glinda drifted to the left and her body wavered as the flame stretched too far. She snapped back into the center.

"How do I end the curse?" Jack barked, straight to the point.

"It should have dissipated when I died." Glinda's surprising and less than encouraging reply.

"It didn't go away, though," he growled. "I'm still stuck here."

"Odd." Glinda floated and turned, eyeing the other people at the table, pausing on Jexy. She murmured, "Your next husband will be part of the Russian Mafia."

"Oh, hell yeah." Jexy fist pumped.

The witch kept turning and frowned at Madame Gizelle. "You've got too much talent for these kinds of parlor games."

To Harper's surprise, Gizelle flipped her a bird. On to Darcy, who gaped in awe. She'd be talking about this for weeks.

The witch pursed her lips. "For the sake of the planet, get him snipped. The last thing the world needs is seventeen of your offspring."

Seventeen? Darcy blanched.

On to Sally. Jack's mother had her lips pressed tight. Glinda paused and stared so long it appeared she wouldn't speak. When she did, it held amusement. "Have you told her yet?"

A mouth already stretched thin almost disappeared as Sally replied, "It's not pertinent to anything."

Harper couldn't help the crease between her brows at the cryptic statements.

Whereas Jack ran out of patience. "Can we get back to the curse? If it was supposed to go away at your death, why am I still stuck?"

The wavering Glinda focused on him, hands clasped in front of her. "I always wondered if there was a reason why my magic was strongest at home. Do you know, outside this property I could barely cast a spark? But here." The wraith whirled, shedding sparks. "Here, I could do anything."

"Why do you think that is?" Harper interjected. "Is it the house? The land? An object?"

"As if I would dare to tell in front of an audience. People are greedy. But I can give you a clue. Look for what's been here longer than anything else," was Glinda's puzzling reply.

Jack exploded out of his wheelchair, bracing a fist on the table as he yelled, "No riddles. Speak plain. Please." The last said on a broken note.

"Very well. You should look at getting rid of—"

The candle suddenly snuffed as Dorothy leapt

onto the table and knocked it over, drowning the lit wick in a puddle of its own wax.

"Fuck!" Jack's yodel fit the moment well.

In the shocked silence that followed, Jack stumped around, muttering about cameras and microphones, back to denying his senses. Sally pleaded with Gizelle to bring back Glinda to finish her reply—to no avail. Gizelle shook her head and stated, "She won't be back."

As for Darcy, she was already helping Jexy plan her next wedding to the man she'd yet to meet.

None of them focused on the reason for the séance. The one railing about being so close to the answer only to lose it, but at least they'd been given a clue.

Something old in this place was the anchor to whatever ailed Jack, and she was going to find it.

CHAPTER ELEVEN

The séance ended with Jack annoyed at first that he'd been wrong. Despite his initial skepticism, without a doubt, he'd been speaking to Glinda. The things she'd known happened between them and no one else. His second irritation came when she'd been snuffed out before she could tell him how to break the curse. Stupid cat, always causing trouble. But the most irritating thing of all?

People were inside his house, and they wouldn't leave.

They ate his trays of food and drank the punch he'd made with fresh fruit and club soda for the fizz. They also chatted, even his mother. Four of women acting as if they were at some social event.

Four too many.

Okay, maybe only three. There was one person in the group he didn't mind feeding, however, she was being hogged by the interlopers. And yes, he recognized it as jealousy that Harper wasn't giving him her undivided attention.

The annoyance at the betrayal of his feelings led to him grumbling, "I'm going to bed."

Harper immediately slipped away from the foursome to join him. "Let me give you a hand."

"I don't need help," he complained as he hit the stairs and heaved himself out of the chair, balancing on the one leg.

"Of course, you don't. Because we know how agile you are when it comes to falling." A flatly delivered bit of sarcasm.

"I'm not going to fall," he insisted, hopping onto that first step, his hand gripping the railing for balance.

"Says you. I have my doubts, and seeing as how the doctor comes to check you tomorrow, how about you forget doing any dumb shit until then," she replied.

"You are ridiculously bossy."

"And you must be tired given how much you're whining. Thought we were past this."

"Maybe I wouldn't be so irritable if my house wasn't infested with people." The truth hissed from him.

"Oh no, you had to socialize for a little bit. You won't die. Just like it didn't kill me."

"You were enjoying yourself," he accused.

"I'm good at faking it. Those kinds of gatherings are exhausting. I try not to have them often, but at the same time I am cognizant of the fact I can't be too withdrawn because, like it or not, I do need some outside interaction."

Her words gave him pause. He stood on his one leg but leaned against the wall for a second, not just to address her but to give himself a break. "You can't convince me that a conversation about the best shampoo to bring out the highlights of your hair is something I need in my life."

Her lips twitched. "Is it the wrong time to ask if I can use yours? You do have a nice sheen to your locks."

He did? He shoved his hand in his pocket lest it try to slick back some lustrous strands. "Sure. Borrow it." She could lather herself with anything in his shower. Which led to him thinking of her in the shower. Naked.

Instant boner meant time to get moving. He whirled and began to hop and balance again, gritting against the strain. Harper remained close enough to catch him if he stumbled. Although, he had his doubts if she could stop him if he took a tumble. Most likely she'd get dragged down with him.

He paused a few hops from the top and admitted defeat. Without a word, she slid under his arm and acted as his other leg, allowing them to reach the second floor.

He plopped into his chair with a sigh. "Thanks."

"It's what I'm here for."

Raucous laughter from downstairs drew their gazes.

"This is not normal," he grumbled. "My mother doesn't laugh." He should know. She came over often, ignoring his repeated demands she abstain. Didn't matter how much he bellowed and complained, she forced him to accept her unwavering love. And what had he done in return?

He'd given her nothing but grief, which led to the uncomfortable realization that he'd never offered her a reason to laugh let alone smile. Such a shit son to a woman who just wanted to care for her only child.

"Your mother has a sharp wit. You should try engaging it sometime," Harper said, as if reading his mind.

"Says the woman who doesn't talk to her dad."

"I have good reason, mostly because he could never be bothered to remember he had a daughter. But you, you've got a woman who would do anything for you. Even put up with you being an asshole."

He grimaced because Harper made a valid point. He'd been a jerk. "Guess I owe her an apology."

"Make her a cake since words are hard."

"She's more of a pastry lover."

"I really liked those little ones you made with the meat and cheese inside."

"Wait until you taste my beef wellington."

"Mmm. Yummy..."

The way she said it had him almost throwing

himself down those stairs to whip her up some right that instance.

More ribald laughter wafted to them, and Harper grimaced. "Guess it's time I got back to the party."

"I thought you wanted to escape."

"I did and do. If I return there will be too much sharing, I will later regret some things I'll say, and that my cousin will use them to fabricate things that aren't there."

"Like what?" he asked.

She had a foot on the first step as she said softly, "We might be in modern times, but they still have outdated ideas about what happens when an unchaperoned woman is left alone with a handsome man."

"What?" Had she just called him handsome?

"Night, Jack. Holler if you need me," she replied as she headed back down to the kitchen.

Leaving him the choice of humping down the stairs in chase or going to bed.

He hit the bathroom first, his mind stewing with the assumption by her cousin that he and Harper were a thing. Had they done or said something obvious? Given how they fought, people should have been assuming the opposite.

Jack emerged from the bathroom to hear laughter from the main floor and the murmur of voices. He was almost curious enough to head back down to listen.

But then thought, what if they discovered him? Tried to make him get involved? Expected him to talk?

Harper claimed she faked being social because she saw it as a necessary evil. Fuck that. Jack didn't see a need to torture himself.

Maybe getting rid of the curse wasn't in his best interest. If he couldn't handle that gaggle of women, what chance did he have if he left this house and encountered a real crowd?

Luckily, it didn't prove to be a problem. The next day, he did something he'd not done in a while. Rolled himself to the fence and stuck his hand over it.

Paw.

Still cursed.

With that settled, he went and made breakfast, an activity that was quickly becoming one of his favorite ways to start the day mostly because Harper sat and watched him. He enjoyed the way her gaze tracked his every move, her arousal a perfume that teased. Was it the food that had her aroused or him? He didn't feel sexy hopping around on one foot and using the single crutch as he preferred to be standing over the dishes as he made them.

She definitely moaned when she ate, and squirmed, which had him pinching his legs tight. Having her around proved to be torture. He wanted her so damned bad it hurt.

But he resisted.

Barely.

A good thing she remained aloof. He might have had difficulty saying no.

After the meal, she shooed him out of the kitchen to do dishes with just one reminder. "The doctor's coming by in the next hour to see how the bones are doing."

"Any chance the casts are coming off?"

"I saw the pictures. It's been a week. I'd say another one at the least"

One more week of avoiding her.

He'd never make it.

The doctor ended up examining Jack in the kitchen since the office didn't have room for the portable x-ray. Dr. Montgomery aimed it at his arm first. Then the leg. The results went to his laptop where he and Harper held their heads close to peruse the results.

He didn't like it one bit. Did she have to stand so close to the man? Montgomery might be married with four kids, but Harper was delectable.

When they did finally part, Jack managed to loosen the fist he'd clenched.

Montgomery clasped his hands together and announced, "You should be good to go a few days after Halloween. I'll be back in a week to remove the cast."

"Or I could do it myself," he grumbled. Even as he chafed knowing he'd have to wear it for seven more days. So few before Harper left.

"You could probably bust out but then I'd be deprived of seeing your smiling mug," Montgomery dead-panned.

Jack scowled even deeper. "Ha. Ha." He actually liked the guy most of the time. He'd been around a few times to check on Jack's health. Even ran tests to see if they could see a biological reason in his blood, semen, or biopsies of his flesh for his curse.

The doorbell rang. "I'll get it. I ordered some groceries." Harper left them alone.

Montgomery felt a need to talk. "Harper says you're looking into the cause of your curse. I'm glad you haven't given up. I've been keeping an eye out for any new tests."

"It's not amounting to anything. We've found fuck all so far," Jack admitted.

"I don't know if I've ever mentioned, but I dated Glinda for a short while."

He eyed the doctor. "Aren't you married?"

"Now, yes, but when I was a young lad in college, the same one you used to attend, I came over quite often for her cooking. And other things." The man chuckled. "She was a fine-looking woman for her age. But damn, could that cat put a damper. Sitting there with a stare, giving you performance anxiety."

"Still does."

The doctor packed his stuff into his case. "A different cat, obviously. She never was without one from what I know."

"Did she ever keep anyone else here before me?" he asked.

Montgomery shook his head. "Not that I know of.

But I was only here for a short while before I moved on to med school."

Odd how the doctor never mentioned this before. Then again, it changed nothing.

Once Montgomery left, Harper insisted on getting takeout for their lunch. He hated the fact she had to leave—*What if she doesn't come back?*—but he wouldn't mind a change from his usual menu.

She returned with greasy spoon homemade fries, onion rings, and a sloppy, thick burger. It was greasy garbage—and so fucking good.

As they stuffed their faces, they chatted about his house.

Harper swallowed—her burger, not his meat—and said, "I am going to check out the attic again. It was protected from you for a reason. The answer's gotta be in there."

To that end, she brought down everything in the space and laid it out in the third bedroom. Even he showed some interest, curious what Glinda had of value that required such a layer of protection. Old clothing that stank of mildew. So much dust. Shoes, some of them missing a partner.

The pictures were more interesting. All of them were in wooden frames with glass over them, the prints yellowed with age. All of them quite old given the lack of color and the clothing styles depicted. They offered a glimpse into the past. How the house first looked, more a cabin than anything. The progression as it got demolished and rebuilt to its current state. Interesting but nothing more.

Seeing all the framed images reminded him of when he first moved in. How the hallway had all kinds of tiny holes, possibly the kind that used to have hooks or nails to hold frames. But why would she have removed these? Did seeing them cause Glinda distress? She had been alone in the world by the time they met.

He pushed a picture of a family standing in front of the place, eight of them plus a dog and cat, to the side. One of the children could have been Glinda. Hard to tell without the wrinkles.

"I'm not sensing anything." At Harper's behest, Jack had held everything at least once—in hopes that the magic from the witch's curse might react with an item from her past—but he'd not experienced a single twinge.

"And nothing you see is reminding you of anything?"

"Nope. To be honest, this pile of old junk seems kind of pointless."

"Then why hide it?"

"Because she was ashamed she hoarded it? Because it was personal? How the fuck would I know?"

Harper felt along the stitching of a man's jacket. "Do you always give up so easily?"

"I spent a decade almost constantly trying to find any way to escape. Excuse me if I'm skeptical you can suddenly waltz in and find it."

"It's okay to admit you're worried that the answer is going to be something obvious. And, yes, it will be infuriating once you realize it was under your nose this entire time, but imagine how it will feel to be free."

"I would be overjoyed if I could break this curse, but it's easier to accept it won't happen than to get my hopes dashed over and over." Annoyed at the presence of all Glinda's sentimental junk and the absence of anything helpful, Jack wheeled himself out of the room.

"Maybe you'll get a Halloween miracle."

He snorted. "Doesn't exist."

She slid under his arm and they started down the stairs. "Maybe you just need to wish to the Great Pumpkin."

"My name is Jack, not Charlie Brown."

"Shh. Admitting you know what I'm talking about shows your age."

His lips curved as they reached the bottom and he settled back into his wheelchair. "And yours."

"I'll be honest, unlike other people, I liked hitting my forties. It became a lot easier to say no to things and ignore pressure to conform."

"I find it hard to believe you'd ever say yes to something you didn't want." She was always so assertive.

"In my twenties, I was a bit more of a pushover. It took me time and practice to get to this point."

"I'm ornery naturally, but in my younger years, I had too much pride and arrogance. It led to me caving to peer pressure," Jack admitted. "It's the main reason why I'm here."

"Your friends made you prank Glinda?"

"I wouldn't say made me."

"Did they call you chicken?"

He cast a glance at her, and she burst out laughing. "I'm sorry! It's not funny!

In that moment, she looked so soft and perfect, he couldn't help himself. He stood and kissed her.

A short peck and he pulled back a few inches to wait.

What had he done?

She huffed in surprise but didn't slug him or push him away. Instead, she murmured, "About time," before she dragged him closer, mashing her mouth to his, and even slipping her tongue into the mix.

He broke from the kiss long enough to remind, "This is probably a bad idea."

"The worst," she agreed.

"We don't even like each other."

"We don't. But it's been a while for me."

"Me too."

"I won't be around much longer, meaning we should be able to avoid the awkward phase that comes when we get bored."

"No strings?" he growled.

"Never!" she promised.

They stared at each other and the next thing he

knew their mouths were latched together once more. Heated, passionate. He wanted more.

He dragged her with him as he sat back in the wheelchair, pulling her into his lap, his chair only slightly protesting the extra weight. His good hand fell to her thigh and skimmed it over the fabric of her pants.

She didn't prove as gentle. She tore the shirt from him. Literally ripped it free, muttering, "I'll buy you another."

As if he cared. She stripped her own top and sat in her bra and pants, looking so sexy it hurt.

She stood for a moment, tugging at his pants and undergarments until he was naked but for the casts and his sling. He slouched in the wheelchair but she didn't return to his lap. She turned and sauntered away, pushing down her slacks until she strutted in bra and panties only. He wheeled in her direction, following his bobbing dick. The living room held a wide and plush armchair, the kind to watch football and seat a broken man but still have room for fun.

The moment his ass hit the cushion, she was straddling him, the moist fabric of her panties rubbing against his hard cock. Her mouth was hot and eager against his. Her hands gripped and stroked his shoulders and arms.

He wished he had two good hands to touch her. One felt like such a tease. But he did his best, using one hand to unlatch her bra. Cupping the full weight, he rubbed his thumb over it until it peaked.

If he'd had two hands, he would have bent her back and taken that nipple in his mouth and sucked. Instead, he was at her mercy—and impatience. She was the one to tear off her own panties. When she straddled him again, his cock strained for her, sensing the pleasure that awaited.

In that moment, she actually paused to murmur, "Last chance to back out."

Never. "I want this more than you will ever understand." The only thing he might regret later? That it took this long to happen.

He reached for her hip and dragged her close. His one hand cupped her full ass. She grabbed hold of him, and he hissed. His hips jerked as he held on. It had been so long since anyone touched him.

She stroked him and drew sharp pants from him as he strove to hold on. Please don't let him spill before he'd gotten inside her.

Wait. He had a moment of sanity. "I don't have condoms."

"I have an IUD. We're good."

He might have died if she'd stopped now. He couldn't help the groan that slipped past his lips when she just chose to slam herself down on his dick. No teasing. Nothing. Just buried him to the hilt. And he almost came.

She remained still for a moment, her channel pulsing around him, silky, molten perfection. She leaned back and changed the angle slightly, drawing a hiss from him, and, even better, giving him a view of her breasts. Heavy with dark and large areoles. He stared, they puckered, and he couldn't resist. He bent to drag one in his mouth. He sucked hard, drawing a cry from her that also tightened her pussy around his buried shaft.

Oh, hell yes. He grazed her nipples with his teeth, teasing one after the other. Sucking them between his lips, biting on the tip, which caused her to clamp down on his dick.

When she shoved at his chest and pushed him back, her mouth once more claiming his, she began to ride. Her ass lifted and dropped, decadent friction to his cock, each slam bringing him closer and closer to the brink. But he held on because he could feel her tautness, how close she teetered. Her hips took on a rhythmic gyration, grinding against his cock, driving him deep. So deep.

He opened his eyes to find her looking right back at him, an intense moment just as they both came. Not only did her eyes widen and her lips sigh at climax, her whole body seized, a tight fist to his cock, milking him. More than that, a sense of something more snapped into place between them.

And then he was back in his body, panting and limp. All over. She had collapsed against him, her cheek to his shoulder, her body intimately meshed with his.

He waited for the regret to hit.

It didn't happen.

Not that time, or the next in his bed. Or the following morning when he actually let her help him bathe, which led to him getting head while sitting on a stool in the shower.

Days passed. Good days of sex and exploration. They went through the house top to bottom. Fucked in every room, some of them more than once.

He tried to not think of the fact she'd leave as soon as the casts came off. They'd said no strings. Why would she stay?

Did he even dare ask?

They never spoke of the future or expectations. Almost as if they both knew what would happen if they did.

Reality would intrude and the fantasy would end.

On the eve of Halloween, though, he couldn't take it anymore. He had to know.

Will she stay or will she go? Alas, before he could ask her, disaster struck.

CHAPTER TWELVE

Harper had been trying her damnedest to find a way to free Jack from his house. She really didn't want to leave him when the casts came off, but at the same time, she couldn't stay. The house was nice to visit here and there, but stuck full time? She'd most likely end up chasing imaginary butterflies like her great-aunt Petunia.

She really liked Jack. Wouldn't mind perhaps continuing what they'd begun. The incredible sex just being part of it. He understood and matched her sarcastic wit. He had no patience for platitudes and stupidity. They were frank with each other except in one respect. What they wanted from each other.

They tiptoed around it, never talking of the future, although every now and then something would slip. He'd say something like, "Wait until you taste my freshly boiled maple syrup. I've got one fat tree and it gives me the best sap." An allusion to spring, many months away.

She'd been guilty of the same. Speaking of the time she'd gone scuba diving and tasted eel for the first time, she'd said, "I'll have to take you to try it."

A bubble existed around their time together and it wouldn't take much to pop. Personally, she would have laid a wager on it being ruined by his mother as she had this thing for random visits. She'd almost caught them the day before in the kitchen. He'd fled to the pantry to buckle his pants while Harper stuffed her cum covered hands in the dough on the counter. She almost died when Sally reached to swipe a bite. Thankfully, Jack yelled, "Toss it out. I just found a weevil in the flour."

Harper quickly dumped the contaminated dough and then scrubbed her hands, biting her lip so as to not giggle. Talk about living on the edge.

After an epic breakfast where she had waffles with whipped cream—and he had her—Jack retreated to his office to work, and she hit the spare bedroom with the items from the attic. Last night, she'd finally begun to flip through the photo albums Jack had dug out. The timeframe of the images spanned a few generations. Unlike present times, few pictures were taken, and years could skip in between. She planned to see if she could use the progression in the albums to sort the pictures in frames. Not that she could have said how it would help, only she had a nagging sense she'd missed something. Something obvious.

The cat tried to take her out on her way up the stairs.

Damned feline. It was as if it wanted to be kicked out of the house. Always tangling in feet or scaring the crap out of her. Unlike the cats on television that liked to be petted, or snuggle, Dorothy preferred to knock stuff over, startle, and stare in a way that seemed to plot death.

Harper went opposite the cat, who headed for Jack's room, most likely to shed on his pillow. She deposited the half dozen albums on the bed and then went to the stack of pictures. Smallest to biggest, the glass plates on them protecting them from damage. She started with the top one. A woman holding a cat in front of the first shack they'd built. A few solemn-eyed children standing in front.

In the next, the same family but much older, along with a cat. Most likely not the same one, given the age of the children.

A noise drew her notice. Was it Jack? Usually, he bellowed if he wanted her attention, pulling a caveman who'd say dumb stuff like, "Woman, your dinner is ready." Or, "Harper, pretty sure I need a sponge bath."

Hearing nothing, she readied to peek at the next picture when she heard brisk knocking.

A visitor? She better answer or they'd get the scowling Jack. She skipped down the stairs to see Jack exiting his office in his chair frowning at the door.

Bang. Bang. Bang.

"Think it's your mother?" she asked of the vigorous knock.

She'd locked the house last night in case his mother tried to swing by. While she had no regrets about sleeping with Jack, she didn't know if his clingy mom would see it the same. A lawsuit claiming inappropriate care—and sexual exploitation—would drain her savings.

Jack's nostrils flared. "Don't open it."

Before she could ask him why, she heard it. The high pitch of Darcy's voice as she said, "Stop banging. It's supposed to be a surprise."

"The door's locked." From Jexy.

But it was the, "We need to be set up before the guests arrive for the baby shower," by Aunt Veronica that froze her.

Harper whirled to stare in panic at Jack, who wore a matching look of utter horror on his face. Maybe they could pretend they weren't home?

Click. The door unlocked and swung open, revealing his mother in a fetching red pantsuit. She smiled wide upon seeing them.

"Ah, there you are. Excellent. We don't have much time to prepare."

"Prepare for what?" Jack asked through gritted teeth as the very pregnant Darcy waddled in with Jexy, Aunt Veronica, and Darcy's sister, June.

"To ready for the baby shower of course," his mother stated matter-of-factly.

"It's not supposed to be until November first," Harper sputtered. She couldn't forget, seeing as how Darcy reminded her twice a day.

Sally waved a hand. "Slight change of plans since I have my monthly lunch with the girls that day."

"Wait, they moved the baby shower date for you?" Harper couldn't hide her confusion. Hadn't Darcy met Sally only days ago?

"Not for me, silly darling. For you. I knew you wouldn't be able to leave my poor Jackie all alone, and yet, how could you miss your favorite cousin's baby shower? Which is when it hit me, Darcy should have it here. Then you don't have to leave Jackie, and as a bonus, no need for a caterer since my darling loves to cook."

"Mother!" His bellow cut through everything, but Sally's expression remained pleasant—if a bit wicked, judging by the glint in her eyes.

"Jackie, be a dear and throw some stuff in the oven. We're going to need some finger foods, but don't worry about the cake. We have a custom one already."

Jack's hands gripped the rims of his wheels tight. "Mother, I'm not whipping together snacks for your little posse."

"Little?" Sally snorted. "Silly boy, this is just the decorating team. The guests will be here in two hours."

He blinked. "What guests?"

Whereas Harper said, "How many people did you invite?"

When the ladies all shared looks, and Aunt Veronica uttered a duh-like, "All of them," Harper sighed. "Prepare for a good twenty or so."

"More," Veronica slyly interjected. "We put out an open invite seeing as how the king's own cousin is hosting."

"What! Why would you do that?" Jack exclaimed as he turned an unhealthy shade of red.

His mother appeared quite nonplussed. "Well, it wasn't as if you'd have offered, and when I heard they were going to do the shower at some coffee shop with thawed baked goods, well, that just couldn't be borne. So I came up with the best solution for everyone."

"How is this good for me?" he roared.

"Because mother knows best," was Sally's inane reply as she sauntered off to help bring in boxes. Some of them were scary, like the one labelled "Birds and Bees" and then there was the Ziplock bag labelled "Pin the Dick." Was it time to admit Harper had no intention of going to the shower? She'd not reached her forties baby shower-free easily. With reason. She had no interest in children, not even those borne by family. Would she send money for gifts? Yup. But she preferred the murdering Dorothy to slobbery, knee-high shriekers.

So yes, she avoided baby showers and birthday parties, but now she'd have no choice. They'd neatly trapped her and poor Jack. He appeared quite shell-shocked.

To help, she pushed him into the kitchen, murmuring softly, "It won't be so bad. We can keep you in the kitchen sending out food. So long as they're fed, they shouldn't get out of control."

"You're talking about people in my house," he whispered. "More than a few. Too many."

"Only for a few hours. And they'll need food," she soothed as she parked him by his island. She headed for the fridge with no idea what he'd need, so she started with eggs and milk.

He wheeled to the pantry still complaining. "I am not a restaurant."

"But you could be. Might be another way to bring in revenue," she teased. "Put you in an apron. Maybe set up a patio bistro outside."

"Not funny," he grumbled.

"You could roar at them if it makes you feel better."

"They'd probably roar back."

She couldn't help her laughter because he'd guessed exactly right. What she'd not predicted? That they would want Jack to join in on the festivities. The party started in the living room, but soon moved to the kitchen and spilled into the dining room, as the guests —almost all lionesses with a pair of wolves in the mix and one tigon—seemed fascinated by Jack. He was like a tortured phantom of the opera, according to cousin Sophia. But much more handsome.

And single.

More than one mama eyed him and shoved their

daughter to catch his eye. Jack scowled, but he also cooked, presenting dish after dish of deliciousness that got devoured faster than steaks at a pride barbecue.

The problem that occurred? The party lasted past the afternoon and into the dinner hour. The snack food disappeared fast and the partygoers were still hungry. Jack went to the fridge and grumbled, "I've run out of ingredients." Rather than see it as an escape, he muttered, "I wonder if I can get a rapid delivery of a few things." For all his complaining, look who thrived under pressure. It probably didn't hurt his ego that they kept exclaiming over his food, declaring it the best they'd had.

However, while he basked, Harper needed a break from the noise. Seeing an escape, she snatched it.

"I'll go get you some stuff. Give me a list." She fled before they could dress her in a toilet paper dress— she'd already done the spoon and egg game, dropping her baby early to end it. Even played "guess the sex" by throwing a dart at a balloon which exploded in pink glitter to much squealing.

The sudden quiet as she stepped outside instantly soothed her frazzled nerves. She felt bad leaving Jack alone, but this refresher would give her the break she needed so that when she returned, she could give him his own retreat. Rather than use his list and bring back shit he had to cook, she'd buy some premade snacks like chips and cookies which would free him from the kitchen.

Past twilight, the streetlights had turned on and provided small pockets of feeble illumination as Harper walked rapidly up the sidewalk. When would the party end? She'd thought baby showers lasted only an hour or two. Long enough to eat a buffet spread, play a few games, open some presents, devour some cake, and done. She'd yet to see Darcy open anything and the cake remained uncut—an inappropriately graphic one with the curly icing pubes framing a fondant-shaped baby being spewed with red jelly.

Who made such a thing? And who the hell ordered it? Her family apparently.

She still couldn't believe his mother had done Jack so dirty, and at the same time, Harper. Making it so she couldn't avoid the party. Sly, Sally. Very sly.

The only good news? No one was getting drunk so they'd be able to drive home, and Harper would be strongly advising that because she couldn't vouch that they would be safe otherwise. It wasn't just Jack who might snap if she didn't get a good night's sleep.

Usually, when Harper travelled, she didn't socialize much. After a day tending her patient, she'd return to her quarters to unwind. On her days off, she would find somewhere quiet to read a book or do nothing at all but nap in front of the television. Things she'd been doing with Jack.

Whom she'd abandoned. He might punish her for it later. Oooh. She shivered in delight. The man had been such a surprise in bed. Not the least bit selfish.

She'd never had so much sex with one guy and not been bored. On the contrary, he looked at her, and she practically tossed her panties at him.

The store didn't have too many people at this hour, and she noticed the Halloween candy shelves were almost bare. Tomorrow was the big day. The anniversary of his prison sentence.

Might have to do something special for him.

A thought to give her pause. Since when she did care about doing special things for anyone?

Less than a block from the house, a grocery bag in each hand weighing her down, she paused and bit her lip. Oh god. Had the unthinkable happened? Had she fallen for him? A thought she might have pondered longer if not for the sudden yelled, "Get the zombie bitch!"

Too late she registered the bat being swung at her head.

Bonk.

The blow left her fuzzy and wavering on her feet. She dropped her groceries but wasn't quick enough to block the second ringing smack which brought on the darkness.

CHAPTER THIRTEEN

The party remained in full swing, with no signs of letting up even though Jack had run out of food. Of more concern, Harper had yet to return.

Perhaps she'd chosen to abandon him to this ravening pack of lions. He couldn't exactly blame her. He wanted to escape too. So much noise. A cacophony created by too many people speaking at once, chuckling, eating, and drinking. Even simple movement caused the ripple of fabric along with the thump and scuff of feet on the floor.

As it became too much, he escaped out the kitchen door to the quiet yard. Was this the world outside the house? If so, maybe he didn't want to escape. He'd gotten used to solitude, although, he had to admit he didn't mind having Harper around.

He glanced off into the distance as if he could somehow see her at the grocery store. Was she still shopping? Had she stopped in a park? The town had a cute area in the middle of it dedicated to grass, trees, an oversized gazebo for events, and a play structure for the young. It was early enough in the evening that he shouldn't have worried. Not here where the crime barely merited the three police officers they had on payroll.

The nagging unease wouldn't be ignored and so he returned to the invading chaos and sought out his mother and without preamble blurted, "Harper's not back yet."

Apparently, not something that worried his mother as she patted his hand and murmured, "I'm sure she's fine. Probably just taking the long way home. She might be people-ed out."

A plausible explanation at the one-hour mark. But by the second? He couldn't help but get agitated. A trip outside in his wheelchair, down the temporary plywood ramp installed over the steps, had him sitting by the gate, staring up the sidewalk as if he could see her. He couldn't smell her. Not in this shape. At the same time, he didn't dare cross that boundary and become the lion, not this early with all the foot and vehicular traffic still out and about.

He headed back inside as some of the guests finally started to leave. The main guests remained to say good-bye. One by one, he asked them about Harper, only to have his fears blown off.

According to Aunt Veronica, "Even as a child, soon

as we had any company came over, she'd hide until everyone left. Getting a hug from that child required a stealthy pounce. Should have heard her scream each time I stole one."

It sounded traumatizing and might have explained why Harper avoided her aunt.

When he spoke to Cousin Darcy she said, "Harp was always disappearing when we were kids. Usually with her nose shoved in a book. We used to steal them from her and make her do something epic to get them back, like the time she replaced Aunt Maura's regular sugar with the kind that gives you the shits. There was nothing to be thankful for when we ran out of bathrooms."

As for Jexy, she was no help. "Forget, Harper. I'm right here, Jackie baby."

Shudder.

He wasn't that lonely.

The party fizzled and the lionesses slunk out, piling into cars and vans, driving back to the city. The presents got loaded into cars and crammed around a tuckered Darcy.

The commotion departed as quickly as it came. To his surprise, though, they didn't leave a mess. The lionesses, under Aunt Veronica's tough eye, cleaned everything. Floors were swept. Surfaces wiped down. Garbage taken out. It might even be tidier than when they started.

Only as they left did he once more waylay his mother. "Harper's still not back."

"Most likely on purpose. How else to stop a party than to run out of food and drink?" his mother surmised. "Now that the gang is gone, she'll straggle in any moment. You'll see."

Only Mother proved to be wrong. A third hour passed without her returning and he worried. Worried enough he put on his robe and stood by the fence on his crutch, putting a little weight on his heel to keep himself balanced. He stared up and down the street, unable to see or hear as well as he'd like. At least the streetlamp had gone dark when he'd activated the switch. He'd long ago ensured certain safety measures for the times he really needed to get out. That included a specialty app that allowed him to extinguish the streetlights on preset paths that would allow him to get out of the town and stretch his four legs.

He didn't have a preset to the grocery store, though. Once he turned the corner he'd be at the mercy of lights and cameras. More people too. It wasn't late enough yet. People closing businesses would still be straggling home. Some restaurants would still be serving. A lion roaming the streets might be noticed.

Jack didn't give a flying fuck. His anxiety wouldn't allow him to stay. He had to find Harper. One thing stopped him.

His casts. The doctor had said they need a few more days.

What if Harper had gotten into trouble?

What if he rebroke his leg and arm?

If Jack waited until midnight, the start of Halloween, he'd be able to keep his casts and he could hobble on his heel. Totally intimidating.

What if she were sauntering back at this very moment?

She needs me. He couldn't shake the certainty.

A glance showed nothing, and so he stripped, dropping his robe, and leaping over the fence, his body shifting jarringly fast. The adjustment from human to four feet took a fraction of a second, and he landed without smashing his face. Nor did his leg collapse. Front or back. But he should try to be easy on them.

In other good news, no one screamed. Hopefully there wouldn't be a video later on to regret.

On the off chance someone was recording... His tail flicked high. He tossed his mane to the wind and strutted. After all, he did cut a fine feline figure.

Hours had passed but he could still follow the path Harper took right to the grocery store a few blocks away. The problem being the many scents all jumbled into a mess, making it hard to figure out if she'd ever left.

Could she have taken the same route back to the house? It would explain the lack of a second scent trial. Had she camouflaged herself so she couldn't be found? It seemed a little extreme but having met her cousins, he could see why she might have wanted to hide from them.

"Franco, I think that guy hit me too hard. I'm seeing weird shit." A yelled whisper caught Jack's attention.

Jack cocked an ear but didn't turn his head lest he startle the speaker.

"Is that a mother fucking lion?" gasped a second male.

"You see it too?" the first guy murmured. "Thank fuck."

"Not really. We obviously got a concussion from that beating. We should go home. I don't think that dude's coming back," the one called Franco stated.

"I can't believe he stole that zombie chick from us. Like we caught her fair and square," the first fellow complained.

"Man, I really wanted to make her pay for pranking us. Not cool making us think she was undead. Halloween's not 'til tomorrow."

Jack's blood ran cold. No wonder the voices sounded familiar. It was the thieves from the other night and with that zombie reference, they had to be talking about Harper. A woman they'd attacked only to be attacked in turn and Harper stolen. It sounded crazy, which meant he needed to have a chat with them. He turned and padded towards them hearing them whisper loudly, "Fuck, the lion's moving. Hold still."

"Shh," was Franco's smart, if loud, advice.

His buddy didn't take it. "Fuck that. Pretty sure noise scares them." The tall skinny one stood and began waving his arms, hooting.

Did he have a death wish?

Jack kept stalking in his direction, his gaze laser focused.

"Abel, you fucktard! You're pissing it off!" Franco exclaimed.

Actually, what set Jack off was the scent oozing off them. They'd laid hands on Harper.

His gaze narrowed and he growled.

"Oh shit! He's mad!" Abel's eyes widened, at least one of them did. The other appeared swollen, just as Franco sported a fat lip.

Jack snarled in their direction and pawed the ground.

"What's it doing?" Abel loudly whispered.

"Getting ready to eat us!" Franco hollered as he bolted. He sped away and Abel followed, the pair of them booking it with Jack on their tail.

He didn't actually plan to harm them. He just wanted to herd one of them to his place so he could change shapes and ask some questions.

Jack came in sight of his house and put on some speed to come in at an angle at the one called Franco, who'd begun to lag. Jack just needed him past the fence and then his fists would handle the rest. Abel saw him coming and veered.

The sudden powder in the air took him by surprise. Jack blinked and huffed, shaking his head to try and avoid it. It burned and he stumbled as lethargy hit his limbs.

Jack sank to the ground and heard hooting in the distance as Franco and Abel eluded him. A man who reeked of cologne stepped out from behind a line of hedges and bent over to grab him around the haunches to drag him. He bumped over some grass, then some paving stones, then up two wooden steps to a deck.

Whoever pulled his body along didn't say a word but had obviously been lying in wait for Jack. A hunter felled by another hunter.

Meaning someone who knew what Jack was. Unfortunate for them. The Pride only had one real rule, and that was to protect their secret at all costs. Which meant whoever drugged and kidnapped him would have to die. Hopefully not with his claws or teeth. Blood in the fur could be such a pain to clean. A crushed neck or snapped spine was much more efficient and less messy. He also liked the cracking sound it made. As to how he knew? There was a time he had issues with game hunters—and his situation left him a tad bit moody. Hunting the hunters that came to town back when he used to haunt the area was therapeutic.

A door slid open on a track, and he was heaved over that lumpy rail then across a tile kitchen floor. He remained drowsy but he could have acted, only he didn't.

Because he'd finally found Harper's scent... in this house. Had this fucker kidnapped her as well?

His limp body was dragged down a hall and into a living room where a woman exclaimed, "What have you done?"

Harper!

He'd found her. The realization sent adrenaline surging through his body. His eyes snapped fully open just as his captor released their grip. Jack bounded to his four feet and roared.

The guy in faded jeans, a plaid shirt, and virtually no hair on his head didn't seem impressed. Nor was he armed.

An easy meal. Jack snarled as he took one step for him.

The fellow, half crouched and beckoned. "Bring it, big boy. I've been wanting to thrash your ass for days."

"Don't you dare lay a hand on Jack!" Harper exclaimed.

Jack chuffed and his tail swished. How cute that she protected him.

"This is between me and the furball," stated the man.

"Jack has nothing to do with us."

Us? Wait what?

He whirled to glance at Harper, seeing her for the first time. She was tied to a wooden chair with neckties, looking irritated but unharmed.

She stared at him and pursed her lips. "I'm sorry, Jack. I didn't realize I'd been gone long enough to worry you."

He uttered a chuffing sound.

"I wasn't trying to avoid you. Blame those idiots from the other night. They ambushed me on the way home."

"*Rawr?*" He should have eaten them when he had the chance.

"I'm fine. I would have escaped if not for his meddling." Her gaze flipped to the man in plaid. "You still don't respect my boundaries."

"I wanted to talk to you." Plaid Man shrugged.

"Not interested. Which you already know. What part of I don't want you in my life do you not get?"

Wait, was this old dude an ex-boyfriend?

Jack barred his teeth. Getting his fur a little messy didn't seem so bad in that moment.

The kidnapper snarled back. "Don't you get lippy with me, boy. I will shoot you."

Not very sporting, and also hard to do seeing as how the guy didn't have a weapon.

Harper didn't appreciate the threat. She offered an icy, "And this is why I went no contact. You can't threaten people for no reason."

"No reason? Ha! I saw you out in the garden together, mashing lips."

Her mouth rounded. "You were spying on us!"

"How else am I supposed to know what's going on with you? You won't answer my texts or calls."

"Because I'm not talking to you," she shouted.

"You're so temperamental!" he yelled right back.

"I wonder who I got that from." She glared at the stranger, which was when it hit Jack. The similarity in expression, the nose, the eyes. Oh shit. This was her father—Dante Jerome. And Jack thought his family was dysfunctional.

"How long will you hold a grudge?" complained Dante.

"As long as I like, considering what you did."

"His mother is way more annoying than me, and he talks to her." Harper's father jabbed his finger at Jack.

"His mother never abandoned him when he was young."

"You know I had to travel because of my job."

"Ha." She snorted. "Excuses. Always quick with them. Guess you need to be a good liar when you can't keep your tail in your pants."

"I'm a man of lusty appetite," boasted her father.

"Glad you had a good time screwing everything you could while I was raised by nannies and teachers."

"I didn't know what else to do when your mother died."

Jack shook his head. A parent was supposed to step up. His mother had once his father passed.

"You should have been a father, but instead fame and whoring were more important to you."

"And I regret that. I've changed. Which you'd see if you gave me a chance."

"No." Harper remained uncompromising.

"That attitude is the reason why I resorted to drastic measures. Although, it should be known that I'd planned to ask you to coffee, but when I saw those two thugs accost you I had to act. Surely me rescuing you counts for something?"

"You then proceeded to drug and tie me to a chair. Like, who the hell does that?"

"First off, the drug wasn't for you but the handsy one over there." Jack got the brunt of that scowl. "I was going to have a talk with the boy about respecting my daughter." As he said it, Dante tugged on the necktie holding Harper's left hand, freeing it.

Harper wasted no time loosening the rest of her limbs while haranguing. "You are a raving lunatic. Jack is my patient, who you might have harmed because his dumb ass came looking for me." Her gaze swung to him along with her ire. "What the hell, Jack? What about your casts?"

He offered a sheepish shrug and pawed the ground.

"I'm sorry you were worried. It seems my getting a concussion wasn't enough. My sperm donor put me to sleep for a few hours with a drug. If you ask me, he's been snorting too many if he thought this would somehow turn into a reconciliation." Harper rose from the chair and put her hand in Jack's mane. "Come on, let's get you home and remove pressure from those limbs."

"You can go, but the boy stays. He and I need to have a chat," Dante insisted.

Harper rolled her eyes. "And people wonder why I have issues. Why must you be crazy?"

"That boy is taking advantage of you."

"Jack is none of your business." She rubbed her forehead. "What will it take for you to leave me alone?"

"Ain't nothing in the world that's gonna stop me from ensuring we have a relationship."

"This is not how to do it!" she exploded.

Jack placed a paw on her thigh to grab her attention. "*Grawr?*" He offered her a solution.

She blinked at him and smiled. "I should let you eat him. But I would feel bad for the indigestion he'd cause."

"As if this cub could take me in a fight. Let's go. I'm ready." Her dad tore off his shirt. He was ripped for his age with scars that showed he'd been seen violence.

She glanced at Jack. "Please excuse my sperm donor. He seems to forget that in the real world, you can't beat up or kill those who oppose you. He also thinks he can force me to call him *father,* despite the fact his only effort when I was growing up was to occasionally send me a stuffy and drop in for five minutes to ruffle my hair and tell me how big I'd gotten."

"I told you I regretted not being more involved," her father whined.

"Good." Harper didn't relent a single inch.

"You will forgive me."

"Not a chance. Now out of my way."

"Don't be like that. We're family."

Harper's fingers painfully gripped the hairs on Jack's head. "Family doesn't have to be blood. It's who you trust."

Her father's gaze narrowed. "So it's like that then?"

Like what? Jack didn't understand.

Harper drawled, "Guess it is."

What? Were they saying what he thought they were saying? Because they seemed to imply…

"I'm leaving now and so are you. You'd better vacate this house you're squatting in and get out of town by morning," Harper insisted as she headed for the front door.

"I'll go for now. If you need me, I'll be staying with Sally."

It wasn't just Harper's head that spun around.

"Wait what?" she asked.

"Sally was kind enough to offer me a place to crash while I'm in the area."

"How do you know Jack's mom?" she asked.

The man offered a sly smile. "We dated just before I met your mother. And before you ask, no I am not Jack's dad, but I could have been."

Kind of gross, but at least they weren't related.

"It's been so nice rekindling our old flame."

Harper gagged. Jack did too.

"I need to go." Harper dragged Jack out of that house into the fresh night air. They both sucked in deep lungfuls before she could manage to mutter, "I need to bleach my mind."

He chuffed hotly in agreement.

She glanced down at him with a gentle smile. "I can't believe you came for me." She cuffed him. "You idiot! Your casts weren't supposed to come off for a few more days."

His amused huffing turned into a chuckle as he abruptly turned into a man which led to her gaping surprise. "The curse! It's broken," she exclaimed in excitement.

How he wished that were true. He shook his head. "More like it's Halloween. For twenty-four hours I get to be normal."

"Then let's make the most of it." She grabbed his hand. "But first, let's get you some pants."

"Aren't we going to talk about your dad?"

"Nope."

"Does he pull shit like this often?"

"This is his first attempted kidnapping," she admitted, dragging him into his yard.

"You really hate him."

"Yes and no. It's more that I refuse to give him the ability to hurt me anymore. Call it one disappointment too many for me to want to try."

A sobering reminder that Jack, too, would be doomed to always let her down. A man who couldn't leave his house couldn't be the man who showed up for the important things in her life either.

How long before she hated him for it?

CHAPTER FOURTEEN

The hate Harper had for her sperm donor clashed with the pleasure at the realization Jack had come looking for her. Never mind she'd not been in any actual danger. She hadn't needed her father's help. The kids dumb enough to knock her out with a baseball bat would have had a fun surprise when she'd awoken and shifted into her lion form to deal with them.

Jack cared enough to leave his home, put himself in danger, and track her down.

Did she thank him, though? No, she called him an idiot for placing his recovery in jeopardy. And it was all her father's fault. What began as a kidnapping by morons turned into an actual kidnapping.

She'd awoken the first time to find herself lying on a couch with the Sperm Donor leaning over her. It was instinct—and pent-up aggression—that made her punch him in the nutsac, which led to him tossing powder in her face. Next thing she knew, she woke groggy and tied to a chair. She'd smelled the heavy cologne even before she opened her eyes. *His* signature to mask his true scent.

"Hey, baby girl." His annoying nickname for her that he had no right to use.

"Fuck off," was her reply. Just as mature as her ignoring his many—many—attempts at contact. He'd been poking at her for years, trying to force a meeting. She'd not replied. Eventually he'd get bored and go away. He always did.

Her sperm donor was the poster model for an unfit parent. A famous opera singer, he travelled the world and fucked his way through cities, leaving at home a daughter who only barely saw him.

In her twenties, he finally told her the truth, that the opera singing and whoring was a cover for other activities. Her father also worked for the CIA as their Casanova who fished for information. Needless to say, the revelation of his real job didn't console a young girl who could have used a parent.

She had no love for the man who kept trying to force it, and his latest stunt hadn't changed her mind. The only good thing that came out of it?

Jack.

He'd worried enough he'd come looking and she'd

never seen anything more adorable. Even as he'd dumbly removed his casts.

Once they got to his house, his naked ass leading the way, she insisted he sit down on the couch. "Take the weight off your leg."

"What happened to seizing the day while we can?"

"It's just after midnight. We have time. Let's call the doctor and see what we're working with first."

He groaned. "You're going to put me back in the cast."

"I'm not the one who played hero."

"I thought you were in danger."

"A valid assumption," she admitted on a sigh.

"Is your father always so dramatic?"

Her nose wrinkled. "He's gotten worse of late. Those years spent in that South American prison really did a number on him."

"Why was he in prison?"

Her lips twisted. "He got caught fucking some important military guy's wife."

"And no one got him out?"

"Did I mention he fucked a lot of wives?" Harper couldn't hide the bitterness.

"Sorry he's an asshat."

"Not your fault. I'm sorry he's banging your mom."

He winced. "Yeah. Let's not talk about that."

She chuckled. "Fair enough." She tried to ignore Jack's nakedness. She'd seen it all, but it still never failed to arouse. Calling the doctor had to take precedence. What if Jack had hurt himself?

Dr. Montgomery answered the phone sleepily and cursed when she told him what Jack had done.

It led to a patient moping as he waited prone on the couch for the doctor's verdict, which turned out to be good.

"Might have been the shifting that helped but looks like you're healed up a little earlier than expected," Montgomery announced.

"Awesome." Jack's first reaction, only as he glanced at Harper did his smile fall.

Had he also just realized what that meant?

Montgomery left and there was an awkward silence as the moment they'd both been waiting for arrived.

"Guess you don't need a nurse anymore." She tossed it out there in the open first.

"Guess I don't. I expect you'll want to leave," he stated softly, looking down at his feet.

"Not really." It was the truth, but the next words out of her mouth surprised her. "I'd like to stay, if you're okay with it."

His frowning gaze met her. "You don't mean that."

"Pretty sure I know what I mean." Did she, though? It was just a few hours ago she was convinced she'd end up chasing imaginary butterflies if she stayed in one place too long. But now that she was faced with it, the thought of not being with Jack seemed like an even worse alternative.

"I'm not condemning you to my prison."

"Doesn't feel like a prison to me," she declared, growing in confidence in her decision as they discussed it. "As a matter of fact, I've never been happier."

"Me either. It's been so goddamned good it hurts!" he snapped. "But it's wrong. I won't have you losing out because of my curse. You deserve to have a real life out there in the world."

"So do you," she found herself hollering in annoyance. Why did he have to be a martyr?

"I want you to be happy!" he shouted back.

"I am happy." She couldn't help but poke him in the chest. "And it's all your fault. Being with you is apparently what I've been needing."

"If you live with me, you'll have to give up your job."

"Or I could work local."

"I'm grumpy."

"Me too."

He stared at her. "You really want to stay?"

"I'm as surprised as you," she ruefully admitted. Harper ducked her head before whispering, "Not sure when I fell in love."

"I think for myself it was the moment you snuck in and scared the piss out of me," he said with a grin.

She couldn't help but shake her head. "This wasn't supposed to happen."

"My mother would call it fate."

Her gaze went to his. "Fate would have let us find the answer to your curse."

"Maybe it never had one, but it found me the one thing to make it a blessing instead."

"You say the sexiest things." She dropped a kiss on his lips but danced out of his reach. "Not yet. Get dressed."

"Why?" he grumbled.

"We can have sex in a bed anytime. But we can only have an adventure outside today. So let's go."

"I'd rather stay in bed with you."

"We can do that for the next three hundred and sixty-four days. Now come on. We've wasted a few hours already."

"I don't like crowds."

"Me either, but we're still going shopping because you need better clothes. Some of your stuff is rags."

"It's called comfortable."

"It's worn out. So let's get some more to break in. Since it's way too early, though, we're going to first find a place that does a nice breakfast. Then we're going for a drive through a swanky neighborhood to gawk."

"You do know there's no mall or decent breakfast places nearby, right?"

"Which is why we're going to the city."

He winced.

She put her hands on his. "We can stay here if

you're really uncomfortable, but I will say that some things are easier to do if you're not alone."

She could see he was torn, but in the end, he murmured, "Let's do this. But I get to choose where we eat. My treat."

"Free food? You're on." She offered a bright smile. Let them have one normal day. Let it be enough to hold her through the next year once the reality of being housebound set in. How long before she craved an outing? Before he resented her for being able to leave? Before she dreaded going back? She could only hope throwing caution to the wind didn't end up in heartbreak.

Despite his initial reluctance, they went out and had a day of fun, using a car that Harper arranged, thanks to his mother. Sally had offered her a loaner if she needed one, and so Harper sent her a text—avoiding the discussion about Dante that they'd need to have at some point.

By the time they'd showered, made love, and dressed, the empty car sat waiting in the driveway, with no Sally butting her nose in for once.

Given Jack didn't drive, Harper did, using his instructions as he navigated her using his phone. They ate breakfast somewhere surprising, a twenty-four-hour place named Eggs-Tra-Scrambly with insane serving sizes. Everything was delicious if cooked in quite a bit of grease.

Jack actually sighed happily as he admitted, "It's

terrible to digest, and way too much, but there is some-thing addictive about all those salty carbs. Once you start, you can't stop."

With their bellies straining, they needed the walk at the nearby outdoor mall, a strip of stores that went in a maze under a mostly open sky. Jack didn't freeze up for long once he realized he didn't feel crowded despite there being people. He bought a few bags of clothes, which he had to dump at the car more than once. The man who didn't want to shop had a blast buying, stop-ping midmorning for a fresh pretzel that had him grin-ning as he chewed.

His playful side remained as they resumed their day, such a change from the dour man. The most shocking part being the lingerie store he entered— without Harper because her cheeks got too hot. He emerged with a bag in hand and whispered naughtily in her ear, "You are going to look delicious in the teddy and matching panties I bought. Can't wait to remove the thong with my teeth."

Happy shudder. She couldn't wait either.

After a busy morning, for lunch they settled on an Italian place with freshly made pasta and sauces that made their mouths sing. The afternoon they spent shopping in some food markets teeming with specialty items that had him practically begging to go home and cook. He could cook plenty tomorrow. When he argued stuff needed refrigeration, she bought bags of ice and stuffed them in the trunk of the car. It helped that this late in October proved chilly, especially once the sun set.

They did dinner at a private and expensive bistro that served Spanish tapas. They groaned their way through the food, then had the most ridiculous dessert from a street vendor: a deep-fried pastry wrapped chocolate bar. So good. Then a movie in a theatre to top off their evening, the big screen just the thing for a wild sci-fi flick with lots of action.

The ride home took longer than expected as construction restricted the highway out of town. They were pulling onto his street as midnight approached.

Harper drove while Jack hung out in the back seat in case he shifted. She kept the pedal to the floor as she weaved around slower moving cars. She didn't let up until she slammed to a stop in the driveway with minutes to spare.

She clutched the wheel and glanced in the rearview mirror. Jack remained Jack. "That was close."

"Yup."

Then because she'd read too many books in her lifetime, she blurted, "Maybe you should see if you're still cursed in case, um, love breaks it."

He stared at her, his expression shuttered. She knew why he looked that way. Fear of having hope.

Before she could tell him not to worry about it, his lips pressed tight as he walked to the fence. He hesitated before he put his hand—paw—over.

Nothing had changed.

Did that mean it wasn't true love? Or that the curse needed something more? She now wished she'd not said anything.

They unloaded the car in silence and headed inside. The groceries were quickly put away, and he remained quiet.

Harper couldn't stand it. "I'm not going anywhere, you idiot."

He glanced at her. "Gee, thanks."

"You know what I mean. What I said outside was a suggestion. Because hey, it could have worked. It didn't. No biggie. I'm not leaving."

"I don't want you to be a prisoner."

"If I need to fly for a vacation, I'll tell you. But I will always come back," she said on a kiss.

He grabbed her around the waist as she lifted on tiptoe, her passion unleashing. All day she'd been wanting him. All day she'd dreamed of touching him.

She tugged at his shirt. It hit the floor. Her shirt followed. Then pants. They shed everything until their bodies could press flesh to flesh. He held one leg up, his hand clamped on her thigh, bringing it over his hip, helping with his angle of penetration. But it wasn't enough to do more than tease given the height difference.

A small noise emerged from her when he grabbed her around the waist and lifted her, turning her so that her back hit the chilly stainless steel surface of the fridge. He held her high enough that when her legs went around his waist, his cock bobbed at just the right height to slip inside.

He filled her. The length of his cock just right, curved at the tip, butting against her sweet spot. A spot that turned hypersensitive when he bounced her. His hands gripped her ass, and he propelled her up and down, pushing deep with each stroke, drawing sharp excited cries.

The friction brought her quickly to a peak that had her gasping for air, her head back, eyes squeezed tight as her body climaxed, tightening and squeezing and fisting him dry.

He collapsed against her, pinning her frame to the fridge. It might have been a lovely moment if he'd not suddenly jerked them to the side.

Crash.

A glance showed the cookie tin kept on the fridge knocked to the floor. The culprit a shadowy cat that glared.

She glared right back. "Why do you keep that thing? It hates us."

"How can't I when Dorothy is just as much a part of the house as I am?"

The lightbulb went off and she suddenly scrambled to get free. "Holy shit."

"What?"

"I think you just solved the puzzle." She streaked from him, naked, racing up the stairs to the spare bedroom. Jack walked in to find her on the bed with the three albums open.

"It's been there all along," she muttered. How could she not have clued in before?

"What?"

She pointed. "Here and here and here."

Jack eyed the dark smudges. Blurry in some images. Clear in others. "What about the cats?"

"Cat. Not plural," she corrected. "It's the same cat in every picture."

"It can't be."

"Then explain why they're the same."

He frowned as he examined each captured feline. Flipping pages to the end, then starting over.

"It's Dorothy," Harper insisted.

"Impossible. Some of those pics are almost a hundred years old."

"Exactly," she declared. "Dorothy is the one constant in all of them. I think she's the source of the magic holding you here."

"But how? She's a cat."

"Is she?" Because cats didn't live to be over thirty let alone a hundred.

"Well, what else would she be?"

"That's what I'd like to know."

As if she knew they spoke of her, Dorothy sauntered inside and offered a baleful stare.

Harper narrowed her gaze on the murderous feline. "Are you the reason why Jack is stuck?"

The cat sat tucked her tail around her lower body.

Jack waved his hands. "Let's say you're right and Dorothy is tied to my curse. What are we supposed to do?"

"You heard Glinda. She says the spell dies with its originator." Her lips stretched as her nemesis hissed, sensing her intent before she said, "We kill the cat."

CHAPTER FIFTEEN

"I am not killing Dorothy." Jack couldn't believe he had to say it.

However, Harper didn't appear to be listening as she cocked her head and entered a staring match with the feline.

"It would make so much sense. Dorothy is the anchor we've been seeking, but what I can't figure out is why she hates you enough to keep you here."

"Assuming it is her."

"We can quickly find out. It will only take me two seconds to throttle her."

The cat uttered a drawn-out yowl.

It led to Jack cocking his head. "I'd swear she understood."

"I'll bet she does because she's demon spawn. Given her attempts to kill and maim, I doubt anyone will miss her."

"You're not murdering Dorothy." Not yet at any rate. Jack couldn't vouch that a few weeks from now, even days, he might change his mind. What would he do to keep Harper?

"Spoilsport. I'd be quick about it."

"Harper." He uttered her name in a stern tone.

"Fine. I won't kill the kitty," she offered a little too sweetly.

His gaze narrowed. "Not specific enough. Say 'I will not kill the creature known as Dorothy.'"

"Fine. I will not kill that demon spawn you call Dorothy unless she tries to kill us first. But I swear, next time she tries to trip me on the stairs, I won't hold back." She mimed kicking a soccer ball.

"Cats are known for being assholes," he reminded.

"Which is why I don't understand your attachment to her."

He blinked. "Is this your way of picking a fight so I tell you to leave? Because if that's the case, you don't have to. I told you to go. You don't have to be stuck here."

"Stop that." She hit him in the chest. "Stop being a martyr."

He caught her wrists. "Stop thinking you can fix this."

"You have to know I won't stop trying."

He crushed her to him, already sensing the trouble his curse would cause, but fuck dealing with it now. He wanted to enjoy the time he had left with Harper before she realized she couldn't keep her promise.

Before she left.

Their lovemaking was fierce the first time, frenzied and desperate, but the second? Sweet and soft, tender and loving. They fell asleep in a tangle of limbs and awoke to a noise on the main floor and a yodeled, "Morning, Jackie. Please tell me you have some coffee."

"Your mother," Harper murmured unnecessarily. The intrusion had them both scrambling for clothes.

By the time they headed downstairs—slightly out of breath and Harper's cheeks bright with embarrassment at almost being caught in bed together—his mother emerged from the kitchen area and smiled. "Ah, there you are, Jackie darling. Look at you, cast free and sleeping in. Must have been a busy day in the city. Did you have fun?"

"Yeah," he replied only to have Harper exclaim, "I'm so glad you're here. I need you to talk sense into Jack. He won't let me exterminate the cat."

To her credit, his mother didn't bat a lash. "I'm sure he has his reasons."

"Because it's a living creature," he exclaimed.

"And?" His mother waved a hand. "Wouldn't be the first time you've hunted small prey."

"This wouldn't be hunting but murder. Dorothy's practically family."

"Who hates you. Let's not forget the roof incident

is one of many that cat has made you suffer," his mother pointed out.

"The toaster in the kitchen sink was kind of suspicious, but cats run through people's legs on the stairs all the time, and once I changed out the gas stove, we didn't have any more problems with the knobs switching on."

"Your cat is a demon," was his mother's dry retort.

He shrugged. "What family doesn't have that relative."

"Don't you care you could end up free?" Harper interjected. "If I'm right, she might be the anchor to your curse."

"Maybe. Or maybe we'll be killing an innocent creature." For all her murderous impulses, Dorothy could have her moments when she wasn't an asshole. Could he really kill something that once a year came into his lap for purrs and pets?

His mother snorted. "If you won't do it, then I will."

"No one is killing the cat. Now is there a reason why you're barging in yet again?" Jack couldn't help his annoyance. This wasn't how he'd expected to spend the day, especially after such a glorious time yesterday.

His mother lifted her chin. "It's come to my attention that you are aware of my affair with Harper's father, Dante."

"Ugh. Can we not talk about that?" He'd yet to

recover from the idea his mom—*Ack*. Nope. Not going there.

Harper stood by his side, equally rigid. "Don't worry. It won't last. My father has never stuck around for anyone before. I doubt he'll start now."

"Actually, I ended it," Sally announced.

"Excuse me, since when?" Dante's sudden appearance in Jack's kitchen startled more than it should have. Apparently, Harper inherited the stealthy gene from her father.

His mom's chin lifted. "Over since last night when I told you we were done. Threatening my Jackie darling. Did you really think I'd stand for it?"

Dante arched a brow. "Excuse me, but don't you mean I ended things for my daughter's sake?"

Said daughter snorted.

"Don't you try and take credit. Once I realized my son was in love with Harper, I told you we could no longer continue," Jack's mother argued.

"And yet you kept visiting me."

Sally fluffed her hair. "To make sure you got the message."

"Four times?" Dante stressed.

Her lips curved. "You can be hard of hearing."

"Only cause you're so loud.

Jack slapped his hands over his ears while Harper hummed really loudly.

"Prudes," Mother opined.

"Guess they're worried we'll get married and make them siblings." Dante waggled his brows.

Harper grabbed a knife and Jack wasn't sure who she'd use it on, her dad or the cat.

"You are not getting married," Jack stated. "I forbid it!"

An announcement that made Dante laugh. "As if I take orders from a boy."

Whereas Sally shrugged. "Wasn't planning to but now definitely won't. Sorry, Dante. My Jackie has spoken."

"You coddle him," grumbled Harper's dad.

"And look at that, he still talks to me," chirped Sally.

That led to Dante scowling and glancing at Harper who almost hissed as she said, "Coddle me and I will gut you."

Rather than be offended, Dante beamed. "Ever think of entering a life in service for your country?"

"So I can run out on Jack and make him feel abandoned? Ha." Harper jabbed a finger at her father. "I won't leave him. I go where he goes."

"Which is apparently only this house. I forbid it!" Dante stated.

"One, you can't forbid shit," Harper declared. "Two, we might have found the cause of Jack's curse." She turned to point to Dorothy. "That cat isn't a cat."

"Want me to shoot it?" Harper's dad pulled a gun from under his jacket.

It led to Jack diving in front of Dorothy. "What the fuck? No."

His mom took his side. Sort of. "Jack's right. Not in the house. Do it outside."

Jack planted his hands on his hips and huffed, "How about we don't kill the innocent cat?"

"Don't you mean the cat that hates you?" Harper clarified.

"I'm sure it has its reasons." He glanced at Dorothy who hissed.

"Want me to strangle it instead, baby girl?" Dante offered.

"I am not your baby anything," Harper screeched.

"Ew, you used to call me that," Sally added to the cacophony.

During that fight, Jack scooped up the cat, who yowled and tried to claw him, but he gritted his teeth against the scratches and carried Dorothy outside. She quieted as he neared the fence.

"Sorry about the talk of killing. I know you and I don't really get along, mostly your fault, but that doesn't mean I want you dead. You should go before someone does something drastic." He'd hate to suddenly change his mind about murdering the cat just to see if the curse would go away.

He set her down by the gate. The cat sat by the opening and stared out at the sidewalk then at him.

"Don't tell me I'm gonna have to yeet your ass out of the nest. I thought cats liked to roam."

The feline stared at him, tail swishing.

"I mean it. You have to go. You can't live here anymore." He grabbed Dorothy, only belatedly noticing how his hands didn't change as he placed the cat on the sidewalk.

Wait. Not a cat.

The shape expanded and grew, elongating to become a willowy figured woman with oval eyes, steel gray hair, an olive complexion, and a slinky figure that wore a very old-style gown.

Dorothy—the non-cat—stretched and sighed. "About time someone figured it out."

"Er, what?"

"The fact I needed to be freed."

He gaped but managed to say, "What are you?"

She smirked. "Sphinx. Captured and bound to this property a long time ago by the original owners. I was supposed to bring them wealth and prosperity."

"Did you?" he dumbly asked, trying to process the odd turn.

"What do you think? They kept me captive. And worse, I could tell no one of my plight. Even got used to it. Glinda did make the most delicious chicken pâté, but even she wouldn't release me."

"She knew you were the source of her magic?"

"More like she suspected. She could make great potions at home, but once she left the house, she was virtually powerless. I tried for a while making her unlucky enough in the house that she'd decide it was best if she moved and took her cat with her."

"A plot that failed."

"It did. The more I tried to convince her to leave, the more housebound she became. Not only that, but she had no one looking in on her. What if she died? It could be years, or decades, before anyone found out. And then you came along. A perfect replacement for the witch. She spoke the words, but I created the spell and gave it intent."

"Wouldn't it have been easier to stand by the gate and meow?"

The woman's lips curved. "Easier, yes, but that wouldn't have been any fun. I did enjoy our time together, Jack. But now it's time I moved on."

With that, she sashayed away, fading from sight. As for Jack, he put his left foot out. Then his left foot in. Then his right foot out, before he crossed through the gate and shook all around. He did a little dance in the middle of the street before strutting back into the house, to hear the fight still ongoing.

He walked in and ignored all sides to bellow, "I took care of the cat."

Instant silence. Harper eyed him before saying, "You set it free."

"How did you know?"

"No blood and your hands aren't covered in hair. Did it work?"

He nodded.

So did she as she muttered, "Should have thought of it. Freeing trapped magical beings is one of the story-book ways to break a spell."

"And you didn't think to mention it before offering to kill her?" Jack demanded.

"Didn't want to give Dorothy a chance to escape in case I did need to wring her neck."

He shook his head. "You're insane. But I still love you."

"Me, too."

His mother gaped.

Harper's father grimaced.

Jack ignored them both to grab Harper's hand. "What do you say we go to dinner tonight?"

"Are you sure we can? There's no rush. In case the spell takes time to wear off."

Rather than reassure, he kept her hand in his as he walked her outside. He stepped past the fence line and lifted his face to the sun.

Harper stared at him. "Are you really free?"

He nodded.

She dove over that fence and just about took him to the ground. He'd never been happier to almost fall in the road because he was no longer bound. He could be with the woman he loved. Forever, if she'd have him.

"I love you," he murmured against her mouth.

To which she replied, "Me, too, and thank the Great Pumpkin for granting my wish. Which reminds me, we owe it our firstborn child."

"Seriously?" He paused mid-kiss.

"No, I still don't intend to have kids, but I would have given anything to be with you. Unlike you who wouldn't kill a cat," she said with a snicker.

"I might have eventually."

"I was ready right away."

"Will you promise to always be like this?"

She chuckled. "Consider this bad attitude yours for life."

He couldn't wait.

EPILOGUE

A *year later...*
Harper and Jack were ready for trick-or-treaters, wearing their Jack Skellington and Sally costumes with an extra gory zombie vibe.

In the year since Jack had been freed, they'd done so much. Not only had they visited Arik in the city, but so far, they'd flown to three destinations: Europe, Alaska, and Brazil. But the place they called home? Oddly enough the house where he'd been trapped for so long. It became their legal address and landing pad, used only for their downtime between travel destinations.

Turned out with his shackles gone, Jack wanted to see the world, taste the local cuisine. The moment they arrived in a location, he would have them eat at an eclectic array of restaurants to improve his repertoire.

Once back home, he then did a chef's special evening at the Lion's Pride Steakhouse in the city. Extremely expensive plated fine dining that soon got a reputation. It led to them travelling for more than just nursing jobs. Jack wanted to expand his culinary experience. While he did his thing, she did hers, and on their time off, they relaxed together. It worked perfectly. Especially since instead of an empty hotel room, they finished each day in each other's arms.

As Halloween neared, along with the anniversary of the curse being broken, they'd chosen to come home. They'd decorated for the holiday and grabbed a few hundred full-sized candy bars to hand out.

The evening proved a success despite her father coming to trick-or-treat as Jack Sparrow. And damn him for making her laugh when he ran off just like Johnny Depp did in the movies. She'd not forgiven him, but she had let him take her out for coffee. Only once. Before even taking a sip, she'd left abruptly. It appeased the little girl in her to show him a fraction of how she felt.

But she knew she wouldn't be petty forever. She'd mellowed with Jack. People still called her the bitch nurse, but she at least liked to think they saw she did it because she cared.

As the night ended with almost all their chocolate bars gone, they went around blowing out candles in pumpkins. Harper extinguished the one by the gate when a flicker of movement caught her eye. A woman dressed in sleek, steel gray head-to-toe eyed the house from across the street.

Their gazes crossed and Harper's lips parted in recognition.

Dorothy.

For a second, she felt a chill, wondering if the feline had returned to exact revenge.

The other woman offered a partial tilt of the lips and disappeared.

Harper couldn't help but stand outside the gate. Long enough Jack came looking for her.

"What are you doing?"

She held out her hands. "Come here."

He joined her on the sidewalk and hugged her tight when her arms anaconda-d him.

"You okay?"

She nodded. Everything was going to be all right.

The Jack-o'-lion's curse was broken which meant they could live their happily ever after.

Well, lion lovers, it seems I wasn't done with *A Lion's Pride*. Will there be another? Guess we'll have to see what my mind cooks up. After all, Dorothy is technically part feline and Dante is an interesting chap.

More books in A Lion's Pride:

Be sure to visit www.EveLanglais for more books with furry heroes, or sign up for the Eve Langlais newsletter for notification about new stories or specials.